CW00495297

MEDIUM CHILL: ISSUE 3

[illegible]
10/11/14
to Mamma & Grandad

"Send my love to Jesus: I am everywhere you go … thank God, this type of shit happens every day."
- Mighty Mohawk Man

Dedicated to: All students – past, present, and future.

Daddy

by Panty Puzzle

Courtney Love And Asia Argento Talk To Joan Didion On The Amalfi Coast

by Constance V. Plumley

For Laura Victoria Albert

"Here take a whole pill, then half of one. Go on! Do like mama says!" Says Sarah, in her blonde hair or wig to her very young son Jeremiah, who she just got back from Social Services. This is, I think, one of the ways that

THE HEART IS DECEITFUL ABOVE
ALL THINGS.

The stories I've heard about celebrity children swirl through my brain at the speed of a candy sugar rush. Joan Didion blooms there on the Amalfi Coast, Asia Argento and Courtney Love are sitting across from her. There is a tape recorder on the table between them. And in the movie of the book, Sarah Says "*I'm all you've got. You better hold onto me.*" Another way that

THE HEART IS DECEITFUL ABOVE
ALL THINGS.

Courtney Love thinks fondly of her witchy, long-legged daughter, and her Alternative Heroine Eyes, and presses the "On" button on Joan Didion's recorder. "*My father, Hank Harrison, the Grateful Dead biographer, he fed me a tab of acid when I was ten years old.*" Joan stares past Courtney Love's head and into the sea, thinking of the mute LSD-fed child in one of her earliest essays. She thought she didn't care at all about that strange stranger's child, but

THE HEART IS DECEITFUL ABOVE
ALL THINGS.

Asia Argento puts her feet up on the table bare, and bluntly says "*Everyone knows how my dad, Dario Argento, put me in all his horror movies even before I had tits. It was normal. It was just art, I didn't mind. It was nothing like Weinstein's grin in that hotel room. Courtney Love is a smart woman. She warned us all about that on the damned Red Carpet*!" Joan Didion smiles, folds her hands, but has no comment at this time. She is thinking of her own daughter, Quintana Roo, and how the bottle made her bump her head too hard, and die. A parent's mind can say "*Yes, you can protect them*!" And the heart will try, too, but,

THE HEART IS DECEITFUL ABOVE
ALL THINGS.

Laura Victoria Albert Instagrams her latest Adventure Meal, thinking fondly of JT LeRoy, the terminator, and of Samantha Koop in that wig. Laura Victoria Albert frowns, then smiles, then types "*I have nothing more to say about JT LeRoy, other than that I don't really miss him much. At least this ink won't fade*." But, we all know that

THE HEART IS DECEITFUL ABOVE
ALL THINGS.

THE HOLOCAUST

by David McCoy

8 3 8 3 9 2 7 8 3 7 6 4 9 2 10 2 9 3 7 5 9 8 2 7
3 8 7 8 9 2 6 7 6 7 11 6 7 8 3 9 5 12 13 5 10 9
6 7 5 6 8 9 13 39 12 9 8 3 4 9 7 5 9 8 13 9 10
9 10 9 4 8 5 3 14 9 8 8 7 6 9 8 7 3 12 9 8 7 11
8 9 10 4 9 8 5 6 3 4 6 5 3 10 9 6 10 9 5 8 8 6
9 8 7 12 8 13 4 5 9 10 6 8 11 2 9 8 3 4 9 11
10 9 31/2 4 5 10 12 9 13 4 8 6 9 10 8 5 7 11
8 9 7 2 6 5 8 13 9 4 5 7 13 4 9 8 5 7 10 12 9
13 4 7 5 9 11 8 13 4 7 5 9 10 8 11 8 4 13 5 7
11 9 8 13 14 5 9 10 9 8 13 4 5 8 7 12 3 9 4 8
5 7 9 11 8 7 3 4 5 9 10 8 6 3 12 14 5 8 9 7 10
9 8 13 4 7 5 9 11 8 3 12 7 4 5 8 7 6 12 9 3 12
8 4 7 5 9 13 8 7 3 12 4 9 5 8 7 10 9 13 8 4 7 5
9 11 8 13 2 7 4 6 13 8 7 12 4 3 6 5 9 11 2 3 8
4 5 7 11 9 10 8 12 7 4 5 9 11 8 2 6 7 3 4 5 8 9
12 7 6 12 4 13 9 5 11 8 7 2 4 3 9 5 8 11 7 2
13 14 9 8 5 7 6 11 8 7 5 6 12 3 6 7 4 5 6 7 11
8 2 13 5 10 9 2 11 13 14 8 9 5 7 8 10 9 10 9
3 2 14 8 5 13 9 12 8 3 4 5 9 10 8 12 7 3 4 15
11 8 12 7 4 3 6 5 8 10 7 12 7 5 9 118 2 3 14.

Ms. Postolento

by Perry Phillips

"You can't tell the same story twice!" I exclaimed *á haute voix* into the auricle of her cherubic ear. Ms. Postolento dropped her violet crayon, paused as if to consider the meaning of thunder, only to retrieve her waxy utensil, continuing to scribble into the day. I gave up tutoring her in petroleum engineering as soon as she began playing with matches.

On hands and knees, I begged her to take up actuarial studies that must begin with rudimentary statistics. Her response was a flat "Non, merci."

I threw out my back moving the empty 500-gallon aquarium that I pushed not-so-gently up against her *bureau à écrire*. She took no notice. Filling the enormous tank with a Python 150-foot No Spill Clean and Fill hose connected to the kitchen faucet two floors down, out the bedroom window, I had a minor mishap during the first hour and water splashed onto the floor around her bare feet. Using her feet like Zakir Hussain might use his hands on a tabla, she paradiddled on the wet carpeting, reveling in the splashing, cacophonous mess. As I drew her attention to the gasping tropical fish in plastic bags on the edge of her *bureau*, awaiting their new home, sadly, one bag, a mixed collection, fell onto the floor and burst open.

The Betta Splendens were writhing anxiously; the rummy-nose Tetras had schooled into a corner upon the largest puddle on the perma-color aggregate, and one of the Clown Loaches lay in reconstituted freeze-dried Tubifex worms. She giggled, in complete innocence, without conscience. Vexed, I went to the basement freezer, retrieved two bags of party ice, and scattered cubes across the floor to simulate a natural disaster. She lifted her head, pushed her Champs-Élysées Eyewear up the bridge of her nose. Eyebrows raised, she turned her head askew to look at me as if to ascertain my true intentions. Then she politely returned to drawing angels frolicking with mermaids.

"Ms. Postolento," I snapped, "You can't continue this

bohemian lifestyle during the current crisis of Late Capitalism. World affairs, with which you'd be more familiar if you took the slightest interest in *Le Monde*, have forced Monsieur le Président de la République to ban non-essential activities. In his State of the Republic Address, our head of state has identified the arts as a non-essential activity. That is to say, we can all live without creativity. Even the greatest works only subtly affect basic bodily functions. Insofar as this is true, I concur: Upon the president's *Chain of the Order of Abdulaziz Al Saud*, Monsieur le Président has proclaimed, 'No More Art,' to which we must all abide to avoid further retributions and continue the present, unending war."

During the brief silence that followed, Ms. Postolento examined my expression for any signs that I might be lying. A twitch of her nose indicated she did not trust me; I had exaggerated about economic opportunities in the past. I held my most serious face—flush-red, nostrils flared—and puffed out my chest. She tested my whole game by giggling and crying out, "Ce n'est pas vrai!" *Oh shit*, I thought, *no respect for authority*.

Omitting the details concerning the House of Saud, I quickly rehashed the whole story about the national emergency, adding some facts about the detention centers for artists, to which she replied, "Ce n'est pas vrai!" I described how even the Little Mermaid was under house arrest, prompting the same retort, "Ce n'est pas vrai!"

Briefly, I gave an overview about the President's men stripping the costume off Mickey's phony human body, linking him to ISIS. "CE N'EST PAS VRAI," she shrieked. She had a tenacious grip, but I sensed a weakened faith in her deepest assumptions. I spoke at length about the financial debacle of Euro-Disney, the unlikelihood of E-D's bailout in the current political climate.

"You can't run a factory on dreams," I reminded her. "Further, the craft of graphic artists has been reduced to sitting at a desk in front of a computer, pushing buttons—a job like any other. Original drawings are no longer necessary," I warned, "You will lap up your own vomit like the rest of the hungry dogs."

Ms. Postolento exploded into a frothy outrage. To gauge the length of this outburst, I measured her reactions to my soft words about the luxury of early retirement, how a lifetime might pleasurably be spent wind surfing, cross-country skiing, or on long walks in the Bois de Boulogne. My suggestions were rejected without due consideration and merely intensified the disturbance. I thought more carefully about the sorts of activities she neglected, but once tried.

"There are millions of things, infinite choices, you are free. You may find you enjoy making popsicles, and then, to show the world you can do it, you might start a little business, small at first, but growing rapidly until, say, one year later, you sell out, buy futures in petroleum…"

"Non, c'est un truc tout bête et qui marche à tous les coups."

"You might also consider saving your monthly stipend to rent a storage locker. You could thereby buy and sell Barbies, either buying new ones made by prison labor in China—in a sense, the passing of a Freedom Barbie from the diligent hands of Democracy Dissidents to the children of the world—Or, dealing strictly with vintage Barbies, going mail-order with a slick catalogue and a good list. Good Supply, Good List, Good Fun."

"You like Barbies?"

"Doesn't everyone?"

Ms. Postolento lightened up when she sensed we might share an interest after all. I seized the opportunity to expound on the benevolent side of Barbies.

"For one thing," I paused briefly for lack of direction, "you can carry one wherever you go."

"Oui, c'est vrai!"

"Also, they make faithful bed companions."

"Oui, c'est vrai!"

"I have also found occasion when, if not for a Barbie, I would have been devoured by demons. I now find myself agreeing with the public that Barbies can be used effectively to repel most types of monsters, just as garlic is used to keep away vampires."

"Me, I have a Barbie, her name is Salomé. She is a bad Barbie, but she does good things. She is the Mommy of All Mommies."

"An important title to confer. Has she transcended Barbiehood?"

"She can do anything…"

"Yes, well, perhaps that's why I had a vision of her on a desert beach lying naked under the stars, without thirst, for all eternity."

"She comes from the Land of Nightmares where everyone is lost."

"Modernity, yes, the Kali Yuga, whatever…"

"Around the halo of the Mommy of All Mommies are fairies who leave light-dust wherever they go."

"Mostly, they sit on the edge of the Halo."

"So you know these things, these things about Barbies?"

"About the Halos of the Mommy of All Mommies, or the diverse uses of the Barbie Politic?"

"After the first fairy came a second one, walking on the light-dust left by the first."

"After one, comes another, as it has always been…"

"The third was a large, human-sized sparkle."

"A what?"

"A medium-sized witch, her name was Francine."

"Are you sure she wasn't a Sparkle?"

"She was! *Comme je t'ai dit!* She was a sparkly witch named Francine who played in the Lost Kingdom. Have you heard of her?"

"No, but I tend to lie around the house, don't go out to nightclubs anymore."

"She doesn't go to nightclubs."

"How can you know? She might sneak…"

"Non! She doesn't sneak!"

"Well, you know her better than I do."

"She is shipwrecked with Mermaids."

"Yep, that's her; saw her at Jaks on Divisidero."

"Non! She's undersea…"

"Deep water, drinks like a fish, as much as a Sparkle can."

"You drink fish; she lives on the Halo of Mommies."

"I occasionally drink Miso soup, and when I do, I remind myself we are all living on the edge of the Halo."

"You are miso kaka; halos are for fairy-mermaids and the President of All Mommies."

"And you are 'the dog barking at its own fence.' And the President of All Mommies is facing term limits."

"You are the dog-fence with miso-kaka and you live in the President of All Mommies' poubelle."

"Well, even if that's true, it's not very nice to point…"

"You are the dog-fence, miso-kaka, Mommy's Mommy poubelle fish-head."

Never had I been so insulted by a six-year-old girl during my tenure as tutor-nanny to the French aristocracy of the Postolento family. I reminded her that most likely the Mommy of All Mommies was above deprecation, that in the purity of her world, no one was dog-fence or miso-kaka. We are, in fact, little sunbeams with dog-fence-miso-kaka forms. She looked at me exasperated, slapping her hand on her *bureau à écrire*.

"Je voudrais une grenadine."

"Ms. Postolento!"

"Maintenant!"

"After how—I don't think…"

"Maintenant! Maintenant! *Maintenant!*

Haunting

by Stew Miller

The thing was decrepit. Its soul clung to the crumbling remains of the structure like bits of long soured meat holds to the bone. Canting listlessly to one side; tired and dying, the barn waited to collapse on the outskirts of the wooded expanse beyond the acres of overgrown farmland.

She wouldn't wander far. She knew to do so would mean risking her health and besides, she had been warned so long ago, "Stray not beyond the ring of pines, my dear heart, for beyond wander madmen and their terrible beasts. Stay close, daughter, stay close." So she had always done; never beyond the ring of pines. Even so, her innate curiosity was still a part of her and she stared, curiously into the land beyond and dreamed of what could be.

The gusts picked up in ferocity and frequency. The ancient nails that bore the weight of the wooden beams and supports cried out in corroded squeals. The twists and grooves of the aged barn made moaning echoes as the storm bore down upon it. It had seen hundreds of these storms during its existence, and despite its aching bones, it would hold through this one.

She awoke with a start then squinted her bleary eyes. Lightening ignited the night making quick shadows play across the walls. She wasn't scared. She knew it was just the weather kicking up a row outside. She had seen many storms and heard twice that they were nothing to fret over. But even so, it concerned her the wind was blowing with such anger and bluster; wind like that left damage and wreckage. She didn't like that because it was ugly. Destructive.

Morning broke with a vast cover of fog that turned the field into a gray, rolling wasteland. Dew clung to the foliage and the previous day's damage was obvious by the sunken boughs of the pines and the snapped limbs of the big maple. The world was damp; the ground spongy and old rain dripped in rhythmic runnels from the barn's sunken roof. The decades-aged wood of the structure's walls was rutted with rot and it held the previous evening's weather in its deep crevasses. The moss-coated chimney glistened with precipitation and the squirrels that called it home sat upon its stone lip and cleaned the dampness from matted fur. A gilded halo slowly climbed over the horizon and threatened to erase the thick mist from its place above the earth.

She stood at the window. Nature slowly left its nightly cover behind and went about its daily activities. She would soon go about hers as well. Silently she glided to the doorway; she still feared waking her mother though honestly she knew it would never happen. Outside now she could see the ring of pines still waving in the morning sun. The ring, she knew, was her boundary. She could never go beyond for there trouble waited that would prove certain doom. But the grounds between her and the pines were hers to explore. She stood outside the door and knew the warming morning sun as a feeling she'd always remember.

As the last of the evening's dew evaporated and the air became heavy, she moved around the grounds staring helplessly at the storm damage. Branches lay strewn about, grayed, broken rectangles of roofing could be found here and there, and bits of tossed detritus hung, caught in limbs and pressed against wooden posts. She stood, surveying the land; land she had come to know as her own. And there, in the distance beyond the pine ring boundary, she saw movement. She glanced again and again the shape moved toward her. Curiosity kept her attention, yet she still knew something was not right. The shape was on two legs.

When she was young she recalled now the day she and her mother moved to the home. They traveled far and came with many other families arriving on the vast, open lands prepared to farm and to live as they always had: with and as a part of nature. The many who built homesteads soon separated the acres of good land into fields growing corn, vegetables, and for a time, tobacco. She remembered the many neighbors she had, the fathers of children with whom she attended school, and the mothers who'd bring pies, host events, and share responsibilities of raising so many children. But the shape of the figure she saw now in the distance -though clearly a man- looked nothing like the silhouettes of people she remembered. She wasn't scared, but she still worried.

She retreated inside, her day interrupted by the stranger walking ever closer. She stood at the window and watched. The dark walking shape slowly became a young man as the shadowy woods gave way to the light from the sun. He was tall, a hunter by the way he walked and carried his gun. She knew a gun when she saw it, but this looked far different from the hunter's weapons she had seen in her younger days. The man looked differently, too. His hair was closely cropped under a cap and he wore dark glasses that obscured his eyes completely. His shirt was mottled in a variety of green and brown hues, his pants the color of the forest, and over them, bright streaks of orange. She had never seen such strange markings. From her vantage point at the window the man looked to be thirty yards away now as he stopped in his tracks.

Brushing a low, damp limb from his path, the man looked down the shallow slope to the old farmland below. He knew he'd stepped off the well-worn hunting trail about a mile or so ago mostly because something caught his senses. A deer? Maybe. Bear? Doubtful this far away from the stream, but even so, maybe. Whatever it was that sparked his curiosity he surely was not expecting the barn before him. Weathered and haggard, its years of disrepair making it swoon under the weight of its own age. That alone was nearly enough to deter him, if it hadn't been for movement.

She saw the man stop. She wondered if he'd seen her. There were curtains, worn and frayed on the windows, but they were not closed enough to obscure the view into the room. And she had moved, slightly, just enough to catch the man's eye. It seemed likely he had, indeed, seen her and that both excited and made her nervous because she was alone. Though she felt safe within the walls, at the same time she knew she was dangerously vulnerable. But the man only looked on curiously and had yet to come any closer. Should she move again? Raise her arms? Do something to let the man know that not only was he in no danger, but that she was there?

The man's nerves were on edge. His heart became one long, continuous beat and it felt like it was caught in his throat. Did he see what he thought he saw? Right then the window appeared empty; darkened and completely devoid of life as the barn itself. And then he saw it again. A shape, human and female, clearly with arms outstretched. She vaporized into view one moment, hazy but quite obviously a female, and then left nothing but a vague remnant as she nearly erased herself from his unblinking eyes. He'd seen movie projectors play films on massive sheets hung on buildings many times before, and each time he'd think to himself how fake and smoky the images looked. Those times reminded him exactly of what he was seeing now. He had never been a believer in an afterlife presence before, but what he had just seen was absolutely unexplainable.

She was certain then. The man had seen her! Her nerves were piqued and she felt something like excitement and trepidation simultaneously. Could she shout to him? Could she tell the man she was there and he was safe? Could she tell him her name? All of these thoughts swirled through her mind as she once again gathered enough of her will to hold out her arms to beckon him.

The man looked on in bewilderment. Once again a cool chill cascaded down his spine and he felt as though his beating heart would burst through his head. The fading image of the girl formed itself from nothing once again and nearly as quickly she was gone. He couldn't catch his breath. His vision swam in blinding pulses. He needed to sit but instead all instincts told him to run. He bit his lip and fought back the desire to flee. His innate curiosity and hunters' senses were on edge; he needed to find out what was happening here. Who was this girl?

It was winter. A vicious, deadly cold wiped out both crops and humanity alike. Families lost children and mothers. Many of the fathers and single men had gone in search of food and it had been months since. The girl and her mother huddled under thick pelts in front of the fireplace burning much of what was left of their wood. The girl looked forlornly at her mother, for she knew her fever had spiked. Her lank hair accentuated an ashen pallor and cold sweat trickled from around her rose-rimmed eyes. "Darling," she rasped, barely able to speak, "Be brave. You know mommy will always love you..." She trailed off into a spasm of coughs. Tears welled and fell on the girl's cheeks.

"I love you, Mommy. Please don't leave me alone. It's so cold and there is almost no firewood left."

Her mother nodded. "I know, my love, and I am so sorry, but this fever has taken its toll and I am dying. You are still well and might yet fight through this dreadful winter. There is little left to eat, yet there is water... and hope. Yes, child, never forget hope. The men, they will return..." Coughs again ended her soliloquy and she sat back tired and weak.

The girl nodded and wiped at her damp face. She knew hope was gone.

And the next morning, the girl was alone.

The girl wished for her mother, to comfort her and offer protection, from everything, from the man. A man arriving far, far too late. The girl shivered. A feeling she recalled all too often. A feeling that shook her those nights after her mother had gone. How long ago?

The man took a step, and hesitated. What if this barn - this house - was actually haunted? What if once inside what he discovered frightened him to his absolute core and what, if then, fear held him to that spot? He was at least able to move out here, but what if? The man shook his head forcefully in hopes of knocking loose the ridiculous thoughts he was trying to process. There were no such things as ghosts, he was positive of that. He was ... wasn't he?

Days had passed. Possibly a week. The girl had managed to survive on small bits of dried meat and a few jars of pickled vegetables. But her rations were now gone. She had run out of wood to burn a few days ago and started throwing anything she could into the fire: a footstool, brooms, chairs, even the legs and supports from both beds. But of that, too, she was nearly out. And worst of all she had fallen ill. She fought hard to stave it off, but her mother had died in the house and even though she had dragged her to the far room until the ground thawed enough to bury her, the sickness was in the air. She had gotten weaker every day and every night broke fever after fever. Things had come to their inevitable conclusion, for her tired, eleven-year old soul.

The man still hadn't moved. It had been a few moments since he'd seen the … what? The apparition of a girl in the window before he realized he had been staring intently at the house. He blinked to clear his vision and felt tears prick the corners of his eyes. He looked around. The sun had begun its slow arc toward the opposite side of the sky and he knew he had to start retracing his steps back to the hunting path. He still was unsure what he saw. That is to say, he knew he saw a girl, but at the same time he knew it was impossible that he'd seen a girl. He turned to leave, glanced once more over his shoulder, and nearly tripped over an outcropping on the ground. It was just a broken limb from last night's storm... except it wasn't. He kicked away leaves with his boot, and knelt to see what it was. And there, nearly blending in to the surroundings, he saw two round, plate-sized rocks right next to one another. The first read: Frances Desmond January 1893 AGE 36, and the other: Bella Desmond January 1893 AGE 11. Both were faded and weathered. The man stood, shaken, and glanced once again back to the barn. He saw no other trace of the girl. He sighed, shouldered his rifle, and quickly headed back, the way he had come.

Heaven on the Way Down

By Dr. Rhonda Baughman

The little boy's idea of heaven was his own room, his own full Lionel Disney train set with official conductor's hat, and his sister Marie there with him, by his side, to help him run the train cars.

But Marie wasn't with him and she never would be again.

Marie went missing the same day they bought the train – he'd been clutching it when the police came to visit the store and take statements. No one took the train set from him while they waited and cast long glances toward him and whispered. And breathed slowly. In and out. This was before all the crying and yelling, of course. Danny tried to breathe with them, like them, and remain still when their voices grew loud.

Danny had looked away for just a few moments to bother his father about additional sets of tracks and the shiny caboose car he had his eye on. Daddy had run into Mr. Bailey and he knew not to interrupt Daddy, but thought just this once would be okay maybe. So he did - and he got a swat for it.

"Go help your sister pick something out!" his dad said roughly. Danny rubbed his backside and wandered off to find Marie. He thought she'd be in the doll section - or the pink aisle - as Danny thought of it. But Marie wasn't there. He looked back at his pops, still deep in conversation with old Mr. Bailey. Danny walked up and down, up and down, and through the corridors of toys he was too young to understand even, in hopes of finding Marie - but she was nowhere to be found.

Danny stopped to look at the war toys - his dad grabbed him from behind, demanding to know where his sister was.

"I don't know," he said. "I thought maybe I would look for her."

"Staring at toys?" his father said angrily. "Forget it. Let's go. She's around here somewhere."

But Marie was not around here somewhere - she was gone.

The first day was the longest and then after a week, his mom and dad stopped speaking and his mother could only murmur. After the first year, as police and well-meaning family and neighbors came and went, it eventually felt as if Marie never existed at all. *And maybe she hadn't*, thought Danny.

He looked at his train set, tempted to play with it one final time before boxing it up - because he knew, once he put it away, he'd not take it out again.

Paleontology

by Perry M. Phillips

Something happens, so it wants to happen again. Since it happened once, it is not unlikely for it to happen twice. Each time it happens, it is more likely to continue to happen, until, of course, it stops. Once it has stopped, it might pick itself off the ground and start happening again or might not.

We tend to shy away from the fact that our species is methodically, yet rather thoughtlessly, causing a mass extinction. However, about one percent of our species' global population is very happy. On the other hand, maybe no one is happy; this commercial euphoria is an illusion created by advertising and sycophantic news services.

Strangely, to everyone's disadvantage, there must be a consensus that a problem exists before we can ask the question, "Is there anything left we can do?" Perhaps our imminent rise and fall should surprise no one and, being extremely optimistic, corporate propagandists continue to expect something better to develop from the toxic dump we create. In the end, something might emerge which would make us look like dinosaurs in our habits and behavior. This popular superstition may indeed have a simple explanation.

We have factories; dinosaurs did not. But what if, say, the Tyrannosaurus Rex had somehow accessed enough ingenuity to cooperatively set up rendering stations to process large plant-eaters like the Brontosaurus? Their energy flow would have increased substantially, and they might have evolved more quickly. Or maybe not. Such cleverness would not have saved them from the cruel-but-brief misfortune of a random asteroid. Consequently, I ask timidly and without much seriousness, "Could we have developed from dinosaurs instead of primates?" Tails, scales, big teeth, and cold blood: impossible! To this day, I share the popular idea that where DNA is concerned, we may not differ greatly from insects, but have no such similarity with dinosaurs.

I doubt these ludicrous thoughts would even be a concern if I had not come across a strange document posted on a telephone pole. The text claimed that we were indeed descendants from the dinosaur in a direct lineage. Excerpts from a document with an NSA header, printed on legal-size paper, 6-point type, exposed an alleged cover-up. According to the document, several fossilized specimens of a rare species, Anthropicarus, were indeed the property of an intelligence agency named FOSIL. The Anthropicarus, like the Platypus, reproduced in an uncharacteristic way. Apparently, the large-brained lizard gave live birth to its offspring. Fossilized embryos were discovered within a well-intact female. It walked upright, had a big brain, was similar in structure to a large ape, but with scales and, initially, a tail. The document went on to say how the tail had always been detachable; it merely fell off forever because it was no longer evolutionally necessary. Speculation was "distasteful for humanity." To make this discovery public would only invite embarrassing comparisons. A minority opinion expressed by a sub-committee document pointed out that, although most reptiles are cold-blooded, they had no historical certainty about the temperature of this lizard's blood. The minority opinion continued by questioning the plausibility of carbon-dating accuracy that suggested this species was alive only a few thousand years ago in an area of recently desertified Ecuadorian rain forest. However, both opinions concurred that this discovery need not embarrass the public.

Naturally, I took it off the telephone pole, folded it, and put it in my pocket. I returned home and lay on my bed and felt the folded flyer in my back pocket. I took it out and studied it carefully with a magnifying glass. The NSA header was official looking. There was a lot of information on one page, as if maybe someone had torn up a bunch of documents in a frustrated rage and then tried to glue them together again.

I mused, "Why not request possible documents pertaining to reptiles or, more specifically, to any sort of Anthropicarus …

The Freedom of Information Act is intended," I said to myself, "for just such purposes," as I filed a request online, sorting through scores of departments, thousands of offices, which were possible repositories, settling on Homeland Security, Office of Biometric Identity. Imagine my alarm when I discovered that the beginning of any FOIA investigation is to open a file on the person requesting information.

The issue required pragmatic instinct. If there were some lizard lineage, it would be rather discouraging for all of us working for our species' betterment. On the other hand, if it was just a false, horrible rumor, then some branch of our national intelligence bureaucracy would likely have enough resources to put me under 24-hour surveillance.

Studying the cryptic leaflet for traces of humor, any sign of a bluff, I set it on my desk. Then I took my disposable lighter from my pocket, a mini bic, laid it on the NSA logo, gave it spin. For everyone's sake, the rare document—true or false—had its momentary flash.

Kayfabe

by Jason Simon

Of course, Lisa was the first to figure it out. As the four cousins knelt on the green shag carpet playing a board game and the nearby television blared professional wrestling, their moms sat around the dining table sipping something they jokingly called "sweet tea" and conversing in an incomprehensible foreign tongue.

"Zeebz zeetz zeemz zeenz zeedz."

The moms had done this as long as the cousins could remember, and, because everything is simultaneously novel and completely ordinary for kids, a secret adult language wasn't really so unusual.

When it was her turn to roll the dice, Lisa leaned in close over the board, now strewn with cards and game pieces, and confided, "I know what they're saying. I mean, I can understand their language."

"Really?" Mark asked. "What are they saying right now?"

On the TV, Hulk Hogan knelt in center ring, the recipient of a brutal beating from "Macho Man" Randy Savage. It looked like this could be the end of his glorious reign as heavyweight champion of the world. The ringside announcers spoke in raised, high-pitched tones barely capturing their disbelief at this shocking turn of events.

"I probably shouldn't say anything," Lisa said. "It's not very nice, and it's about your dad."

"Come on," Chris said. "Just tell us. We don't care."

Lisa thought about that for a minute, considering whether or not to give up her advantage as sole translator of this alien code. Finally, she said, "They call it Carnival. My mom learned it from a friend when she was little. Then she taught it to your moms so they could have a secret sister language grandma and grandpa didn't understand. Now, they use to it to gossip in front of us about adult stuff."

Mark looked surprised. "Wait. Are we seriously carnies?"

"No," Lisa laughed. "My mom's friend learned it from her family. Maybe *they* were carnies or con artists or something. I don't know."

"OK." Jeremy said. "So how does Carnival work?"

"It's really easy," Lisa said. "You just insert a 'eez' sound into each syllable of a word, so a word like *carnival* becomes 'ceezarneezaveezal'."

"How do you say *dog*?" Chris asked.

"Deezog."

"How about *Batman*?"

"Beezatmeezan."

"Oh, OK."

This was a minor revelation. The cousins had long grown accustomed to their moms buzzing like bees whenever they got together but had never really considered that these sounds might actually convey meaning.

Lisa rolled the dice and advanced six places. She collected a card but didn't share whatever ominous fate it foretold.

"So, what are they saying?" Mark asked. "I mean we know our parents fight all the time. They think they're hiding it from us, but they're not."

As Lisa decoded that Mark and Chris's dad was always drunk and couldn't hold down job and had his buddies over every day to smoke pot in the garage, Jeremy found his attention drawn to the television. Hogan seemed to be rallying. Although Macho Man continued to rain blows upon him, the champ held his head high as if unfazed. Clearly the tide was beginning to turn.

"Your dad didn't go bear hunting in Alaska last year," Lisa said. "He was in jail for a week."

Chris noticed Jeremy's shift in focus and said, "Here's where the Hulkster stops feeling those punches and shakes his head like *no way, man*. Then, he'll throw Macho Man into the ropes, leg drop him or body slam him and then pin him. It'll be all over soon."

Just then, Mark and Chris's dad entered the room as the women continued to drink their tea and gossip in Carnival. He had long, curly hair and was dressed in a mesh muscle shirt and patterned athletic pants. He said, “There you witches go again with your gypsy curses.” The women laughed amiably as he leaned down and kissed Mark and Chris’s mom on the lips.

As he left the room, the women immediately started speaking in Carnival again.

Lisa said, “She just said she’s going to leave him as soon as she has enough money.”

“Woah, really?” Mark asked. He and Chris looked momentarily stricken. “They seem fine. They were just kissing.”

“Sorry,” Lisa said. “I knew I shouldn’t have said anything.

On the TV, Hogan staged the exact reversal Chris had predicted. As the champion clenched Macho Man to lift him for a finishing body slam, the two wrestlers exchanged a quick look and what seemed to Jeremy to be a nod. He wasn’t sure whether or not he’d imagined it, but, soon enough, Hogan slammed Savage to the mat for a quick three-count and thunderous applause from the audience.

Lisa won the board game as usual. As the cousins picked up the cards and tokens and put the board away, Jeremy stopped to watch a minute of Hulk Hogan’s post-match ringside interview with Mean Gene Okerlund. Still champion, he was larger than life in his victory yet humble in his evocation of training, eating vitamins and being true to one’s self and country in securing this monumental comeback.

The moms emptied their glasses and sat silently for a few seconds. They were smiley and sort of glazed-over from the tea. They then rose from the dining table as though through an unspoken accord and moved to the kitchen to begin final preparations for dinner.

“You kids hungry?” Lisa’s mom asked.

Jeremy’s mom said, “This pot roast has been cooking all day. It should be good and tender by now.”

Finally, Mark and Chris’s mom said, “Go tell your dad dinner will be ready soon. Ask if his friends are staying. They’re in the garage.”

Jeremy’s mom shot her a look and said, “Teezell theezem

theezay beezetteezer heezold theezeir breezeaths eezout theezere."

Across the room, Lisa's eyebrows raised, but of course no one needed a translation just then. Yet rather than point out to their moms how much they now understood, the four cousins played along and helped set the table for dinner, complicit as adults.

Troubleshooter

by Tom Mattevi

It never ceases to amaze me - I can be so calm and collected one moment and then BAM! without warning, I'm a nervous wreck and always for the same reason: a woman. Yep, I can stare down ghosts, ghouls, vampires, werewolves and any assortment of demons and devils but let a woman confront me and I'm a quivering lump of protoplasm with no more sense than a scorpion dancing in the desert at noontime on the sunniest day of the year. And I can guarantee you that no amount of holy water, wooden stakes, and silver bullets are going to save me. Never has … never will.

Her name is Donna. She breezed into my office just as I was about to break for lunch. She said she needed my services. All it took was one look and I knew she was going to get whatever she wanted from me. She was what could only be described as my curse. Just the type I always fell for and then just waited until that exquisite moment when she would tear out my still beating heart and then, as I watched, throw it onto the ground and dance on it until it ground into dust.

Wait, you're probably asking yourself: *Just who is this guy?* Sorry, I guess I should have covered that before. I assumed you knew me. The name's Diore. Matt Diore. And I'm a professional troubleshooter. That's right if someone or something is giving you trouble all you have to do is call me and I'll shoot it. I mostly work in the field of the esoteric and exotic. Supernatural is just natural when you take away the super. Okay, so it's not the classiest saying in the world but it keeps me from going hungry.

Anyway, this lady comes in and says she has trouble and needs me to help her fix it. Now I know right away when the biggest trouble had just walked into my office and if I were smart I would just shoot her and move on, or better yet shoot myself and be done with it, but no, I bade her take a seat.

She told me she believed the spirit of a former lover, who has since passed beyond this veil, (having had its heart torn out and danced upon no doubt) was plaguing her. I told her I could take her case but my rates were not cheap. She removed her coat and I approved her credit immediately as I could see she had tremendous credentials, and her assets weren't half bad either. She gave me the particulars of this particular case and when I said I wasn't sure I wanted the case she offered to give me a retainer but since my teeth are pretty straight I passed and asked for some cash instead.

We decided it would be best if I went out to her residence that night and scope out the situation. She lived at 666 Beastdale Circle, just south of Antichrist Avenue and north of She-Devil Street. I knew the area well. Many of my clients and most of my dates live in that neighborhood. In fact, I suspect at least one street had been named for my ex-wife.

I arrived at sundown as per my instructions. Donna met me at the front door and asked me if I wanted to case the joint. I told her I only smoked tobacco but that I would like to look around the premises once she put that in its case. She accompanied me as I toured her home. It was nothing to get excited about. There were two bedrooms, one bath, a kitchen, dining room, living room, and a rumpus room. She said rumpus would not be back as it had the night off. I was glad as a rumpus can get in the way of an investigation. There was a full basement made up of two rooms. One was finished and served as a family room but her family must have been very small as so was the room. The other room in the basement had several broken windows and large holes in the walls. She said it was the wreck room and I couldn't argue with her. We went back upstairs. I asked her where the apparition had appeared. She told me that it had always appeared in one of the bedrooms. I re-examined the two bedrooms paying close attention to the doors and windows for future reference. I told her I would spend the night and see what I could see. She told me I could stay in the spare bedroom and she would sleep where she always slept but I convinced her it would be better if she slept in the other bedroom rather than the back seat of her car where (as she put it) all the action is. She went to bed around 11:00 pm. I went into the spare bedroom but I knew I wouldn't sleep tonight.

Around 2:00am I heard Donna scream, and I knew the game was afoot. I was right – and there it was! A large apparition fondling her tootsies. He was a podiphile. I knew how to handle this. I ran back to the spare room and grabbed my valise, opened the clasp and rummaged until I found my can of Desenex. I ran back into Donna's room and gave him a shot …! To no effect. What the … Suddenly, I noticed it was the wrong can. Okay, so I have another itch too - sue me. I ran back to my valise and got the right can and ran back in and sprayed him. He immediately shrank away. I kept shooting him until he withered away to nothing. Donna sat up, stunned for a moment, and then leapt off the bed, threw her arms around me and started kissing me all over. Finally, when she stopped, she thanked me for ridding her life of that terrible curse. She asked if it was gone for good and I said if it ever comes back we know what to do, don't we.

She slowly lay back down on the bed then looked at me with those come hither eyes and bid me to come over closer to the bed. I did. She asked me if I would remove her nightie. I did. She then asked me to remove her bra. I did. She then asked me to remove her panties. I did. She then asked me to never wear her clothes again.

The next morning, she paid me and I left but I had a feeling I'd be seeing her again soon, in fact I was certain of it. As soon as I got back to my office I readjusted my telescope and waited for nightfall. Yep, her curtains were still open, so I knew I'd be seeing her again.

Way

by David McCoy

The Second Ticket

by Fred588

Inez would ordinarily have taken no notice of something like a receipt for a day at Psychic World. Kim, her roommate, had a perfect right to go where she wished. If a day wandering unarmed in a deadly jungle was what she liked, then she could do that. She mopped up the spilled coffee - she had a bad habit of eating at their desk - and put the receipt back in Kim's drawer. But something caught her attention.

"Oh!" she exclaimed to herself. "*Two* tickets!"

"*What would Kim be doing with a second ticket*?" she thought.

Kim tried to dismiss the whole thing from her mind. She trusted Kim. They had been together for five years. But Kim clearly had purchased two tickets, for the same day. *Could Kim be having an affair*?

The tickets were for the following Friday night. Inez resolved to go to Psychic World herself on Friday and find out what was going on.

Friday afternoon she called from work and left a message for Kim on the answering machine that she was going to be very late getting home and not to expect her before midnight. Then she called Psychic World and arranged for a ticket of her own.

The entry portal was ready when she arrived and, since she had been in the Psychic World Jungleland once before for a guided tour, she was able to go right in.

As soon as Inez entered the jungle she realized finding Kim would not be easy. The place was huge and moving around quickly was dangerous. She might easily run right into a giant snake, a nest of alligators, or a quicksand bog if she was not cautious. But, at least she'd had the guided tour and knew a few details about what to expect.

Inez reasoned that Kim would probably not be involved in

any of the organized activities or games the Psychic World staff offered, such as snake wrestling or *Quicksand Roulette*. Kim might go for some such things but she thought it was unlikely. *Pirate Territory* also seemed unlikely. Kim would find that intriguing but that was something she would do alone, if at all. Most likely, Inez reasoned, Kim would be in the open jungle.

For nearly two hours Inez wandered through the open jungle, searching. Everywhere she went there was a sense of danger of the most terrifying sort, yet it was all very exciting. Once she had to stand motionless for nearly ten minutes while a gigantic snake crawled across what vague path served as a trail not fifteen feet away. Another time she walked right into a quicksand pit but realized her mistake in time and backed out after one leg went in halfway to the knee. It occurred to her that the fondness with which some ex-soldiers talk about experiences in battle might be similar to the love many Psychic World customers seemed to have for the place.

Then, she heard Kim's laugh. It was unmistakable. Creeping cautiously toward the sound, she quickly came to a clearing. And there was Kim, chest deep in the middle a of bubbling pit of clay and in the embrace of their friend Jean. Neither seemed the least bit alarmed that they were sinking in quicksand either; they were much too interested in each other than in worrying about the mud.

Inez was as surprised as she was disappointed. The idea of Kim having another lover had occurred to her but she never thought it could really be true.

"*Kim, no! how could you do this!....*" she thought to herself. A tear welled up in each eye.

Inez did not move and said nothing for several minutes. She merely watched in horror and Kim and Jean sank deeper, still locked in embrace. The mud rose higher and higher, covering Kim's shoulders and nearly covering Jean's. Mud was caked all over both girl's arms, necks, and face from having been smeared on by the other. There was even quite a bit of mud in their hair.

Gradually, Inez's hurt turned to anger. She moved forward to confront the two lovers.

"Kim," Inez cried out angrily. "What are you doing?"

Kim and Jean looked up, though they did not seem overly surprised or upset at having been caught.

"What's it look like we're doing?" Jean responded in a matter-of-fact tone.

"We're just sinking in quicksand," Kim answered in a similar tone.

Inez's mouth dropped open in surprise. "Just sinking in quicksand, my Uncle Sue!.... You're doing a bit more than that."

"Well, not really. It's not what you think," said Kim innocently.

"Oh no?" answered Inez incredulously. She knew there could not possibly be any way to explain what she had seen. "What is it then?"

"Well," said Kim confidently. "You see, this is not really Jean."

"Who is she then, Jean's evil twin? And what difference would it make if she was?" Inez prodded angrily.

"She is no one," answered Kim. "Just a projection. Not a real person at all."

"What?" Inez gasped. Inez did not believe a word of what Kim had said, but then Jean simply vanished. She was looking right at Jean as she simply dissolved into air. Clearly she had not gone under.

"Oh!" Inez went on. For a moment she was embarrassed at having suspected Kim. Then she realized Kim was not entirely innocent either. Her anger was much reduced but she still felt some sense of having been betrayed.

"What are you doing out here making out with a projection of Jean?" Inez continued. "Not to mention in the quicksand."

"There's a simple explanation for that, too," Kim answered.

"And it is?" Inez prompted.

"I'm a projection too!" Kim responded.

"No!" said Inez with disbelief.

"Where did you come from then?" demanded Inez.

At that moment Kim dissolved into air, then reappeared standing on the edge of the pit. She was just a few feet away, still totally covered in mud.

"I must have come from your mind," answered Kim. "From your fears and suspicions."

"Damn!" said Inez reflectively. "I think you must be right. I saw those two tickets and I began to suspect you, ah. the real you might be having an affair."

"I'll bet there is a really simple explanation," said Kim.

"I hope so," said Inez. "The affair came from inside my own mind."

"Yes," said Kim. She paused for a moment, then added. "The affair came from inside your mind. From your fears. But where did the quicksand come from?"

Inez stood there speechless for several seconds.

Then Kim went on. "Could it be that you'd like to try it? To jump right in or maybe be pushed in … and go all the way … under?"

"Well, yeah," Inez admitted, as much to herself as to Kim. "I kinda always did have a fantasy about that. I do want to do that, I think."

"Good!"

Inez was startled to hear Kim's voice, but from a different direction. She turned to see Kim, the real Kim just a few feet away and coming toward her rapidly.

"Kim!" Inez called out, opening her arms to the side, offering an embrace.

Instead of embracing Inez, however, Kim placed her hand against her chest and shoved her backwards, into the mire.

"What? Oh!" Inez gasped in surprise. "What are you doing?"

"Don't play games with me, Kiddo," Kim answered. "I saw the whole thing."

"What?" said Inez with surprise.

"So you've always had a fantasy of sinking in quicksand, have you?" Kim teased. "You really want to do it, do you? Well, you're going to now."

For a moment Inez was focused entirely on the mud rising rapidly all around her. It was thick and very heavy. It seemed to be sucking her down inexorably. Everything about it was terrifying, yet she was not panicked. Then, suddenly, there was a huge splash and Kim was beside her in the mire. They embraced.

In little over a minute Inez and Kim were both neck deep in the mire and still sinking rapidly. In less than another minute the mud would swallow them both.

"One thing," Kim gasped as the mud reached her lips. "The other ticket was for you."

"Were you going to ask if I wanted quicksand?" Inez wheezed, beginning to choke on the mud.

"Knew it all along-phghmpph" she said to Inez, then to the quicksand, and then to nothing.

Eugenics

by Robert Beveridge

Your decisions: whether a hornets' nest can resemble an orgasm, paper or plastic, the particular shade of umber you prefer for your toast. T or C, T or C, T or C, G or A. There are five hundred seventy-six billion, six hundred fifty million, three hundred ninety thousand, six hundred twenty-five possible combinations to your teenage diary's lock; you've ransacked your mind and come up empty, so it looks like brute force is your sole option. You wonder, as you try yet another combination that begins with A, whether they would still let you on the 21-25 squad, even if your thirty-second birthday passed last week.

We picture a top, upside-down, in an endless spin. We take a second top, place it point to point with the other. When we pump the crown, our top spins in the opposite direction. We can sit and watch them for hours. Sometimes we do, in the same way we stare at the cannon bone, how something so small tapers down to the hoof yet still supports the endless weight of the gallop.

(in the slot, the number
in the wind, the toy)

When the Applejack hits, the devil tattooed on your thigh jumps up as if to dance, but instead offers advice: it's time to pack up and head for Lagos, became Nigeria's premier director of industrial safety films. You're still stuck in the As, but at least you've gotten as far as ACAAMGGRYT. Not that it's opened your diary. You wonder what the perfect aperture is for that once-in-a-lifetime pull-back shot of a forklift atop the bluff outside Bodinga Chilgori, but then you remember that Bodinga Chilgori is one of the few places on Earth where the weather report indicates the likelihood you will develop a migraine that day.

The crackle in your ankle identical to the crackle in your lungs. The air is cooling, the northern hemisphere in its inevitable descent to winter. Fine, save the particulates. You yearn for a pair of glasses in reverse, one where you can use the lens to focus the smoke, return it to sunlight.

(I have never been
your mentor but I
can still find pieces
of copper behind
your ears)

Burger or nuggets? Fries or apple slices? Apple juice or milk? Boy or girl? Do you always just tell them it's for you?

Somewhere along the way you noticed that Survival Research Laboratories stopped being a performance art group and became a business model. But hey, that's nothing a quick jump from the suspension bridge that's always just over the horizon wouldn't fix.

(after a period of silence the world begins to turn again)

In Need of Nepenthe

by Ilaria Easom

Sitting on the sofa with her legs folded under her, Laziras stared longingly out of the window and up at the trees. She had an albino Belgian Malinois curled up on her lap, her fingers running subconsciously through Blizzard's soft fur. Twisting, she huffed and let gravity pull her backward into the couch, one hand behind her head, the other across her stomach. Blizzard squirmed to lay between her and the back of the couch. Laziras wrapped her arm around the albino dog, pulling him closer and burying her face into his fluffy coat. She closed her eyes and let her head rest against his. There was no more redamancy required between them. They were inseparable. *Life without Blizzard would be no life at all,* she thought.

The door swung open with a bang and Blizzard leapt over her, barking and panting excitedly. She didn't have to open her eyes to know who it was. "What do you want?" She grumbled into the empty place where Blizzard had been moments ago. The familiar wall of anxiety had already made contact, her heart pounding in her chest, stomach clenched and a mild headache forming.

She felt someone grab her hand and yelped in surprise as she was yanked from the comfort of the cushions. Clothes were shoved into her chest. Looking up, she locked eyes with Sage, the person who had messaged her mere minutes ago. Never in her life had she seen the girl so serious, so worried and so excited at the same time. Her face showed nothing but concern, but her eyes showed a spark of excitement.

"Right," Sage turned back to the door and took Blizzard's black collar and blue leash that hung on a hook next to the door. Crouching down, she fumbled with the clasp around the snow-white dog's neck as he wanted nothing but to prance around and play. "You get dressed. I'll meet you in the car."

Laziras was more than just a little tired, she was full on drained from worrying, panicking and obsessing over the things that didn't deserve that attention. She was in a serious need to purge the burden she carried around every day. She was scared to leave the house once in a while and some days, it made her impossible to deal with. They tried a therapist, but an inability to explain her thoughts and feelings got in the way, leaving her unable to express herself, unable to do anything other than answer simple questions, peace of mind nowhere to be found. Fear of people and society haunted the insomniac every waking hour, the paranoia and anxiety everlasting. Despite being only fifteen, she recalled a time of adventure in her life where fears and anxiety did not prevent her from the eternal desire to run wild among the creatures of the world, her beloved Blizzard loping beside her. All she did now was relive those adventurous times through daydreams, sitting around all day imagining the life she lost, the life she missed. She missed the challenges the world could provide her, the riddles, the mystery, the thrill of the hunt. She missed being the wild, reckless girl everyone knew and loved.

Stunned, Laziras wasn't sure which part of her it was that obeyed Sage's command, but she knew one thing was for sure; she had been stuck in her oblivion for far too long. She wasn't vivacious anymore. The slightest familiar feeling of anticipation crept into her heart, a wavering smile attempting to pull at her lips. Her body, used to being in a constant state of being just barely awake, felt like lead as she moved, pulling off her pyjamas and smoothing the new clothes over her fragile figure. Every day, her routine consisted of staring into nothingness and dreaming. Clearly, that was about to change.

She'd said it before and she knew it to be true; Sage was almost psychic and knew exactly what she needed. They've known each other for so long, it was no wonder that a sixth sense had developed between them. They were practically sisters. Sage always took such good care of her and it hurt Laziras to know she could never repay her when it came to the stuff that truly mattered. She had pushed away everyone she loved because she couldn't bear knowing that she would weigh them down. She wanted to set them free, but it was Sage who was freeing her. Despite knowing that her fears were insignificant when compared to the vastness of the universe, she still felt herself becoming less meaningful to the world day by day. So many people had stopped questioning and just accepted, they had moved on; something she could never do alone.

Something that had been dormant for far too long was coming alive again. She examined herself in the mirror; a white hoodie with black sleeves and a black hood, 'I SPEAK FLUENT SARCASM' on the front in big black letters, the fabric thin enough for the cryophilic she was. The torn black jeggings weren't something she would usually wear, but then again, she only wore pyjamas for the past two years. The black boots may have been a little over the edge for her, but something about the extremity of the colour contrast made her smile. For a time, all too short, worry-free joy flooded her system until the familiar rush of anxiety crashed down, resuming her sense of reality. Her smile instantly fell and she bit her lip.

What if she couldn't do this? What if she let Sage down? What if-

She closed her eyes, leaning against the bathroom counter with her elbows, back arched and her head hanging between her arms. She clenched her hands as tight as she could, counted to ten, then let them hang limp. Moving her neck from side to side a bit, she felt it clunk back into alignment. She tried again, making a fist tight enough for her nails to break her skin had they been in the position to. She counted to three then to five as she breathed but it wasn't enough. The voices in her head wouldn't leave her alone. They wouldn't stop putting her down. "Shut up!" she growled at her reflection. "You'll never know if you don't give it a try!" She could feel her throat growing tighter, her eyes stinging with tears as she forced the words out. There was always the voice at the back of her head, telling her things like this, but words and actions speak bigger than thoughts. "This isn't you. You're not this frail, this...fearful! Get a grip!" She pounded her fist into the bathroom counter to drive the point home.

Surprised by the effectiveness, she instantly recoiled,

hands covering her mouth as she gasped at her own behavior which was now completely inhuman and unknown to her. She couldn't help but imagine that this was what it felt like to let loose a stream of curses and feel better after, her heart beating fast but not in fear; in excitement. Maybe she was ready to move on, to go back outside and explore. The place that made her really who she was, it was never this place, it was never home. It was always with those she loved, the world outside that everyone was nervous to venture out into. That didn't change. She did. She had built up a wall around her that she hid behind, debilitating fears leading to emotional numbness.

Laughing at the outburst, she returned to the living room cautiously optimistic. She reached the doorway and placed a hand on the doorknob, her foot on the threshold, poised to step outside. Sage and Blizzard were waiting patiently by the car outside, watching with interest and encouragement. Laziras brought her feet together, lips parted to allow for the change in her breathing as fear sunk its massive talons into her again. She looked up at Sage. She didn't know if she could do this. She hadn't left the house in what, to her, felt like years.

Once again, Sage read her mind. Within seconds, her friend was holding her hand tightly, standing close at her side. "On three. Come on, I'll do it with you." Laziras said nothing but took a shaky breath and nodded. She didn't just want to do this now, she had to. She *needed* to get out, to break through the walls.

"One," Sage counted off. "Two."

"Three," Laziras breathed. Stepping across the threshold of the house was like passing through a force field, like shining a light on the creatures that went bump in the night. The first wall broken by a single insouciant step.

Blizzard seemed overjoyed. Prancing around, he hopped up on his back legs and pawed at the air with his front, making the girls laugh. As Sage opened the back door for Laziras to get in, Blizzard jumped in as soon as the gap of the door was wide enough for his body to fit through. Sticking his head back out of the door, he bit Laziras' sleeve to pull her in. In the driver's seat,

Sage twisted and handed over a bandana. "It's a long drive. You can sleep if you want to." At nineteen, Sage was allowed to drive, but age wasn't an issue when it came to the bond the two shared.

Laziras shook her head. She could do this. "I wanna watch."

The car slowly built up speed, driving down the dirt road leading to Laziras' cabin in the woods, rolling down the window for Blizzard to stick his head out. Sage glanced up at the rearview mirror, peering into the backseat. "You're not as nervous as I expected you to be."

Laziras shrugged, staring out the window at the buildings passing by, a small smile tugging at her lips. "Guess it helps when you know you're not alone." She looked up at Sage. "Can I ask you a question?"

"Shoot."

"Why are you doing this?" Sage raised her eyebrow, eyes flicking up to the mirror again then back to the road. "I mean like," Laziras sighed, exhaling forcefully through her nose and sticking her tongue to the right between her teeth and her top lip. "Why are you doing this, actually, you know," she gestured around the car. "This."

Sage smiled. "Do you remember when I was going through depression and I was cutting myself with a safety pin?"

"Yeah," Laziras' eyes were half closed and she seemed half asleep, the heel of her left palm pressing into her cheek as she rested her head on her hand. Regardless of how tired she was, her memory was always on point. It was safe to say Laziras remembered the severely emotional conversation they had all too well.

"I needed your help then and you need my help now. You're practically my little sister, Lazi. I don't need to return a favour to help someone who I care for and who cares about me." Glancing up for a third and final time, she wasn't surprised to find that Laziras had fallen asleep.

Unaware of how much time had passed, Laziras felt herself being shaken awake, her vision filling with the image of her friend as Sage stood between her and the world outside the car. “I don’t want you to see.” Sage smiled and gently tied the bandana around Laziras’ eyes, taking her hand and guiding her carefully out of the car to their destination. She stood behind her. “Three,” She untied the bandana. “Two,” She lowered it, knowing Laziras' eyes were shut. “One.”

Laziras' green eyes fluttered open. Instantly, she took a step back, tears spilling as the last wall shattered like ice under a hammer. It was beautiful. Mesmerized, she forgot the world. The sky was a blend of intense colours, the sun all but sunk below the horizon, illuminating the sky with all shades from gold to pastel pink, the darkening night sky above. The indigo ocean crashed beneath them at the base of the cliffs, the inky depths churning and entrancing.

Sage was truly the definition of good and beautiful in a person. She had been through a series of hurricanes and tornadoes herself, but each time she’d always pulled through more polished, the event having been nothing but sandpaper to refine who she was, to make her stronger. The comprehension behind Sage’s reasoning was unanimous between the two. Laziras had been shown something that no other person would understand. An overwhelming sense of forgetting the world washed over her as she watched the pull and push of the tide. This was ataraxia; pure emotional tranquility.

Scars

by Steven Santana

I arrive home from another miserable day in high school, throw my backpack on my bed, and shut my bedroom door. My emotions are all over the place as I simultaneously want to yell and cry. The tormenting, and being pushed around was a daily occurrence for me, but today was different. I try as best I can to just ignore it but, it has broken me. It is a constant shouting in my mind, like a song playing over and over, lyrics and melody never changing.

"No one cares about you, FAT ASS!"

"Go jump in traffic you idiot, it's not like you'll be missed!"

"A girlfriend?! hahaha yeah ok, maybe if she's ugly or blind!"

I just want it all to stop. I finally know how.

No one is home so I don't have to worry about getting caught, and I think it's time to get ready. I head to the bathroom and grab a loose razor blade from my dad's shaving kit. I sit at the edge of the bed, fidgeting with it between my fingers. I take a deep breath as I press the cold metal against my wrist and wince as the razor makes its way between my flesh. A single drop of crimson emerges as I guide the blade down towards my elbow. The immense amount of pain takes over and I let out a yell.

"OH MY GOD! WHAT ARE YOU DOING?!"

My mother came home early and I didn't hear her enter. She rushes to me as more crimson streaks down my arm. Panicked, she grabs my wrists. Pain shoots through my body and I scream even louder. At that moment I look down, ready to pry her hand off, and see no blood, no razor, no cuts. Nothing but ...

Scars.

A drowsy voice whispers to me, "What's going on?"

My wife is propped up on one arm, her head leaning

against my arm. I'm sitting up on the edge of the bed, hands trembling slightly. I must've woke her up.

"I'm sorry babe. I didn't mean to-", I say to her without even turning my head, voice breaking slightly.

She gently turns my head to meet hers and she notices my eyes are a bit watery.

"Another nightmare? You gonna be ok?" she asks.

I look at her and nod slightly, wiping away the last of tears I was unaware of shedding.

"Yeah, I'll be okay; just need a second to calm down".

I didn't realize it at first, but I'm gripping my wrist tightly. She smiles at me and tells me how much she, and our son love me. She uses her soft hands to loosen my grip before rolling back over, taking my arm hostage till I'm up against her spooning.

She traces her fingers over my scars and kisses them gently.

"You are a great man and they can't hurt you anymore. You love and are loved in return. Don't ever forget that", she whispers.

I feel like I'm broken, still trying to mend all the cracks and fractures in my mind. I think about how lucky I am to have my own family, and how they give me a reason to go on. A small smile comes across my face and I drift off to sleep still holding the most beautiful girl in the world.

Free Candy

by Tom Mohler

The rusted-out cargo van sat parked down the road as the six children stood huddled together behind a large elderberry bush. Aida peered through the branches, eyeing the old, windowless jalopy.

"I heard there's a whole a mountain of candy inside that van," said Aida, turning back to her friends.

"Yeah," said Ellie, "but my Mommy told me that the man that drives it is a pervert."

"What's a pervert?" asked Becca.

"A pervert," Nicky explained, "is a grown-up that likes to touch kids. At least, that's what my teacher told us during stranger danger safety week."

"Touch? Like a high-five?" young Bruce inquired.

"No," said Nicky, "like a bad touch."

"Oh, like on our private parts?" Charlie asked grimacing.

"Yeah," Nicky replied, "and my Dad told me not to go anywhere near that van. He said that the guy in there wants to take us away and hurt us— that he's a bad guy. He only has that candy in there to trick kids like us into getting inside with him."

"If he's a bad guy, why don't the police get him?" asked Aida.

"I don't know for sure," said Nicky, "but I think he has to get caught doing something bad first."

"But if they know he's bad," Ellie asked scratching her head, "then why do they have to wait until he does something bad to punish him?"

"Yeah," said Aida, "that doesn't make any sense. If everyone knows that he wants to hurt kids, then why doesn't somebody stop him before he can?"

"Maybe we could stop him," said Charlie, punching his fist into his palm.

"Yeah and get all that candy for us," Becca exclaimed wide-eyed. "I bet there's a ton of it in there."

"Oh yeah, and how do you think we'll be able to do that?" Nicky asked. "We're just a bunch of kids, not the Teen Titans or something."

"Hmm," said Aida, rubbing her chin, "I think I have a plan."

***

Later that evening, just before dusk, Aida approached the rear door of the candy man's van. She looked to her left and then to her right and then reached up and began knocking. Loud rummaging emanated from inside and then a raspy voice called out, "Yeah, who is it? Whada'ya want?"

"Hey there, Mister," Aida replied in her sweetest voice, "I heard you have some candy in there that you like to give out to kids. I was wondering if I could have some. I sure do love candy."

A pair of bloodshot, beady eyes appeared behind the steel security screen covering the van's rear window. They looked down at Aida, narrowing maliciously. The raspy voice replied, "Yeah, little girl, I've got a whole boat load of candy for a sweet thing like you." The door swung open, revealing a middle-aged man wearing a torn-up flannel and ripped blue jeans, holding a large bowl full of all sorts of delicious treats. "You can have all the candy you want," the man said, holding the bowl out towards Aida. "All you have to do is hop in." He smiled at her, itching his dirty, unkempt beard. "Come on."

"Wow," said Aida, "that sure is a whole mess of candy. I'd love to have some, but my Mommy said not to get into cars with strangers."

"Yer momma's just being over protective," the man said, licking his lips. "I ain't gonna hurt ya."

"I don't know," Aida said, taking a few steps backwards, "maybe I should just go."

"Don't be silly, little girl," the man said, setting down the bowl and stepping outside, "we can just sit in here and talk and eat candy together. Doesn't that sound nice?"

"I do like candy," said Aida, taking another step back, "but I still don't know."

"What's not to know?" the dirty man asked, stepping towards Aida and holding out his hand. "Come on, just get in. We can be friends."

Aida cocked her head to the side, a mischievous smile upon her face, "But I already have friends, Mister. They like candy too."

"They do, do they?" the man asked.

"Yeah," Aida said. "They love it." She glanced to her left and right and then yelled, "Now, guys! Get him!"

On Aida's cue, Nicky came charging around the side of the van, swinging a pipe wrench into the man's knee. The man let out a howl, grabbing at his leg, as Nicky reeled back the wrench and swung again.

Aida ran over to the sidewalk to pick up the baseball bat she had left there in wait, as Ellie crawled out from under the van and began shooting staples into the man's butt and back with a staple gun.

"Ahh!" the man cried out. "You little fuckers! What the hell?"

The man shoved Nicky to the ground and was about to stomp him out, but then Charlie ran out from around the other side of the Van and started wailing on the dirty old bastard with the nail puller end of a twenty-ounce claw hammer. The hammer impaled deep into the man's skin with every strike, blood spurting out on each backswing.

As the man pivoted towards Charlie, raising his fist to deck the kid, Becca sprung from behind a nearby bush brandishing a crowbar. She stormed the pervert, swinging wildly, bludgeoning his back and sides. She swung the two-foot mass of steel into him over and over again, fracturing his spine and dropping him to the ground.

Aida grabbed her aluminum baseball bat and ran over to the downed molester. She stopped with a skid, yelling, "Batter up!" and swung it right at his temple. The blow caved in the side of the man's dome with a loud crack, knocking him flat onto the pavement.

The rancid pedophile lay twitching in the fetal position, blood pooling around him, as the children continued to beat on him mercilessly. "This ought to teach you not to be a bad guy!" Aida shouted at the top of her lungs. "Now give us the candy!"

"Yeah, you dirty old pervert!" Charlie yelled, still going to town on him with the claw hammer. "Give us the damn candy!"

"Don't forget about me!" little Bruce hollered, running down the sidewalk, lagging behind as usual. "I want to help too!" As Bruce hurriedly approached, the other children looked at what he was holding, and all took a step back. Bruce pulled a Zippo lighter out of his coat pocket and spun the striker wheel, springing it to life. He raised up an aerosol can and sprayed it through the open flame, engulfing the bloodied pervert with a stream of chemical fire. The man's raggedy clothes ignited, turning the dirty sack of shit into a beaten down human torch laid out on the side of the road.

"Whoa," Nicky said, "that's gotta hurt like the bees!"

"Yeah," said Bruce, huffing and puffing and pulling out his inhaler, "he's toast!"

As the balled-up pedophile lay smoldering, wheezing his last miserable breaths, Aida stepped over his scorched husk and grabbed the bowl of candy out of back of the van. "We got it guys! Let's go!"

The children all rushed off, scattering throughout the neighborhood, as the dirty old candy man lay burnt and bleeding out at the rear of his rusted-out rape van.

***

The children all sat in a circle in their club house, surrounded by a pile of candy wrappers, the now nearly depleted bowl of treats at their center.

"Dang, Aida," said Nicky, "you sure weren't kidding

about that guy having a ton of candy!"

"Yeah, Aida," Ellie chimed in, "that worked out great! I've eaten so much candy that my tummy is starting to hurt. Best day ever!"

"You're telling me!" Bruce exclaimed with a mouth full of chocolates. "I just hope my Dad doesn't find out I took Grandpa's war lighter."

"We really messed that guy up though," said Becca, unwrapping some salt-water taffy. "You think he's going to die?"

"Who cares," Charlie replied, chomping on a licorice twist. "He was a no-good bad guy that wanted to hurt kids. That dirty old man got what was coming to him. Besides, this is the best candy I've ever had!"

"Well you know what they say," Aida said with a smile, "candy won tastes a whole lot sweeter than candy earned!"

Gun Land

by Jason Simon

John wakes up in the morning in his two-bedroom flat in Beijing and sits down at the kitchen table sipping his first cup of coffee before work while scrolling through social media updates on his phone. He expects the routine highlights: Aaron ran 8 miles today in preparation for that marathon in Orlando next week, Jeff wishes to remind us via a reshared comic strip that he is vegan and thus morally superior to the rest of us, Michelle's two-year-old son achieved another milestone today of dubious merit and Beth just can't even, alright; she's over it. He's sure his own posts are equally banal, and that's just fine. This is his lifeline to the States and to most of the people he cares about, and such triviality is endearing.

He laughs to himself at how living halfway across the world can make even shallow small talk feel comfortable, like home.

Today, however, is clearly that *other* kind of familiar. There's been a mass shooting somewhere in the US, and his network feed is chock-full of the histrionics associated with the now-too-frequent aftermath of a violent tragedy. Scott is calling for increased mental health screening because gun control is a stupid, liberal fantasy. Jeremy feels obligated to remind us that we wouldn't be facing this if we hadn't taken God out of our schools at some undefined moment in the past. Angela shares a list of how much money each member of Congress receives in donations from the National Rifle Association. Sarah wants us to shove our thoughts and prayers up our respective asses.

"Jesus…"

John's boyfriend Ning joins him at the table with coffee and an everything-bagel with cream cheese on a small purple plate. "Did you hear?"

"Yes. I'm reading about it now."

"Your country is crazy. I really don't understand it."

"What's to understand? People get killed everywhere. Some crazy guy here stabbed a woman to death with a samurai sword, right outside the Uniqlo over on Gongti Bei Lu."

"Yes, that's true. A person murdered another person two and a half years ago, and you're still talking about it today."

The details of the shooting are unspectacular. The man, a loner about whom details are still emerging, accomplished neither a new body count record nor distinguished himself in any notable way as a multiple killer of humans. He used a semi-automatic rifle with a high-capacity magazine and spoke little during the attack. There was a restraining order on record against him from an ex-girlfriend, who was not listed among the dead. Acquaintances always found him a little unsettling but couldn't imagine that he would do something like this. He was white, male and in his twenties. Same old shit.

***

John arrives at work about an hour later, dreading the morning office banter, in which he—the only American in the high school English department—will be appointed de facto spokesperson for all 320 million of his countrymen. Sometimes, he has no trouble characterizing or, at least, contextualizing the beliefs and viewpoints of people back home, even when he doesn't necessarily share them. He can explain the sharing of federal and state powers and the innovation that emerges regularly from the free-market private sector. On some level, he can even illuminate the prevailing if misdirected anger that lead to Hulk Hogan or whoever-the-hell being the current US president. When it comes to guns, however, he feels just as lost as the assorted Brits and Aussies and Canadians he works with.

"You do realize you're basically the only country on Earth that deals with this. That every other country has figured out a way of addressing this issue."

"I'm aware."

"Well, shouldn't that tell you something."

"It should, yes."

"Then why are your leaders so obstinate?"

"Because…freedom?"

"In Australia, voting is compulsory, which prevents demagogues with only fringe minority support from being elected."

"Yes, I've heard that before."

"You had 90 million registered voters who stayed home binge-watching Netflix instead of doing their civic duty."

"It's a problem."

"In the Canadian parliamentary system, the majority party needs to cooperate or at least create a coalition with other parties to even form a government. They can't just come in and start immediately destroying what's come before them."

"Yep."

On this day, he's just glad he teaches the first block and won't have to spend as much time in the office. The students are less smug and accusatory when they ask questions about what's happening in the world. They're genuinely curious but a lot more tolerant because they've been taught to be through a diverse and cosmopolitan curriculum.

A particularly precocious boy named Feng stays behind today after 10th grade English.

"Mr. McDonald? Did you know anyone involved in this shooting?"

"No, this one was in a different part of the country. Thank you for asking that, though. That's very kind."

"Oh, OK. So, are white Americans so obsessed with guns because they're afraid of black people rising up against them?"

"Uhh…yeah. I think that's a pretty big part of it actually."

"Really?"

"Oh, I don't know. They'd tell you it's for personal security and as a safeguard against an out-of-control government taking over. That it goes back to the American Revolution and that resisting tyranny is an American tradition. I can't pretend to know what they're actually so afraid of. Probably black people."

"Did you grow up playing with guns?"

"No…uhh…I've never even held a gun. My dad supposedly had a handgun somewhere, but I have no idea where his hiding places were. We certainly didn't have weapons lying around the house out in the open."

"Do my questions offend you?"

"What? No, definitely not. I understand that you're curious, and I understand why. I'm sure the whole idea of gun culture seems very foreign to you."

"Are you afraid when you go home to the US in the summers?"

"No, not really. The odds of getting shot are still pretty low, especially where my family lives. I do think I'd be afraid to be a teacher there, but that probably has just as much to do with combative parents as it does with school shooters."

***

When he gets home from work, John lounges on his sofa while sipping a bourbon highball and browses his network feed again. As is expected, people have hunkered down into their ideological trenches and continue volleying shots over no man's land. Or whatever the online equivalent of that is. His old university professor shares a meme about how armed toddlers kill more Americans every year than Islamic jihadists do. A high school friend who's been in and out of jail most of his adult life offers that we're not spanking our kids enough or raising them right anymore, not like when he was young. A Dutch former coworker points out that this is karma for the damage the US's military presence around the world has inflicted on innocent people for decades. Multiple people speculate about the most recent shooter's political party affiliations as though they all expect him to have been fundraising and hanging candidate placards in his spare time while descending into homicidal madness and as though this revelation will provide the ultimate victory in these drawn-out culture wars.

"Fuuuck…"

Ning's key turns audibly in the front door. He works at a bank down the street and typically gets home an hour or two after John, which gives John some time to unwind from the day before having to freshen up to join him out for dinner.

"Has it been a whiskey-drinking kind of day?"
"Why-Not Wednesday, I'm calling it."
"So, it's like Might-as-Well Monday?"
"Yeah, you've got the idea."

***

The next morning, John sits nursing a catastrophic hangover. In theory, he should be able to stay out half the night drinking and dancing at his age and be perfectly fine in the morning. In practice, only Ning is able to do this while escaping the brutality of a next-day workplace hangover.

In John's hazy memory of the previous night, he and Ning went from dinner first to a trendy cocktail bar, a place where the staff shushes you for getting drunk too loudly on their copper-cup concoctions, then to a tiny hole-in-the-wall Latin salsa club, where they worked up a sweat gyrating with a few straight female friends, and finally to a quiet hole-in-the-wall pub, where a young, blonde woman, maybe American, strummed a guitar and sang earnestly in a breathy alto that gave the sense that each of her vowels was being slightly misrepresented.

He remembers having had one of a few recurring dreams he's had for as long as he can remember. In this one, he is maybe eight years old and playing in the basement of his childhood home with his little brother Billy. Their sister Janet is probably asleep in her crib upstairs. John is painting his black skateboard red using paint from cans he's found hidden under the steps, but he's accidentally making a mess all over the cement floor. When he looks at Billy, he sees that the poor kid is covered in red and worries that their parents are going to be furious about finding paint everywhere. Then, Billy takes off running upstairs. John puts down the skateboard and goes after him, trying to stop him from tracking paint upstairs and making everything worse, but he can't find his brother. He just sees red footprints all through the kitchen and living room, and then he wakes up.

And later at work, he pays the price all day long for the previous night's misadventures. At lunch, he stops by a table where students, including Feng, are selling pastries to raise money for the funerals of yesterday's shooting victims and buys a croissant to settle his stomach. He's touched that they're being so empathetic and globally minded, even if that money could be better used to help orphans or migrant workers here in Beijing. *Baketivism.* He resists the cynical urge to dismiss all their good intentions.

***

On Saturday, John wakes up around 10:30 a discombobulated horror-film zombie and stumbles out to the living room sofa. He's hung over again after an eventful Friday night. Far more disciplined, Ning has gotten up early and gone to the gym already for an hour or two of cardio and weights. Again, John reaches for his phone to see what's been happening in the world since he last checked, and, again, he regrets it.

The news today hits closer to home. At the middle school he once attended where Janet's son, John's nephew, is now enrolled, a 12-year-old brought a rifle to school in his backpack, assembled and loaded it in the first-floor boys' restroom and then shot himself. At this point, no one knows whether this was an accidental self-injury and part of a foiled rampage killing or a public suicide attempt. There are rumors of explosives in the kid's backpack, but these are still unsubstantiated. Some people are claiming he just had bottle rockets and other fireworks. The shooter's prognosis remains unclear, but no one else has been injured. Later, it will be more or less accepted that the boy, who died of the self-inflicted wound, had had Columbine-style objectives of mayhem and mass murder.

As John scrolls, he sees that the school was on lockdown for a few hours and that the kids of some people he knows were affected. One friend wrote, "It's hard to explain what it's like to get a phone call at 8:00 AM from your daughter's school telling you there's been a shooting involving a kid in your daughter's grade and the school's on lockdown." Another wrote, "My elementary school kids were just dropped off at home. The high school and middle school are on lockdown. This is my worst nightmare."

He checks to see if Janet has posted anything. At 7:15 she wrote, "Thank you for all the messages and prayers today. Will is safe and at home. He's asking a lot of tough questions tonight. Going back to school on Monday is going to be tough."

Generally reticent to engage on social media beyond airport check-ins and Thailand beach vacation photos, John joins the fray. He shares a satirical news article about how the United States can think of no solution to gun violence despite being the only country routinely dealing with it. Next, he posts an infographic about the gun murder rate in the US vs. other developed Western countries.

Then, he writes, "Today's school shooting happened in my hometown at the school I once attended. If my life had taken a different turn, I might be working there now. And looking over my shoulder. Have I mentioned lately how glad I am to be living and working as a teacher in places where this isn't a concern?

"Yesterday, my hometown newspaper posted an opinion poll asking how people feel about armed guards and metal detectors in local schools. People were strongly in favor. I read it and thought, 'Who's paying for that? School levies? Your property taxes? You cheap bastards won't even pay for an updated science wing.'

"Fix your shit, America. It's getting harder and harder to explain you as I travel the world interacting with people from places where the idea of regular mass shootings is as inconceivable as alien invasions. You're embarrassing yourself."

He stays online for about an hour as 30-or-so friends "like" his post and a few comment "Well said" or "Amen". "What has happened to our town?" one asks. "I tell my son to 'be safe' now before he gets on the school bus in the morning. I shouldn't have to say that. I should say 'have fun' or 'make some new friends' when he leaves for school," another says.

The feedback isn't all positive, of course. Some friends debate the finer points of bump stocks and gun safes with him. Others muddy the waters with tangents about regulations of automobiles and pharmaceuticals. Other people join in to argue with those people. Some people are just obstinate dickheads and engage in proxy battles about abortion or the president. There's a lot of back and forth about whether gun control is a solution or a band aid or, conversely, whether arming teachers is a solution or a band aid or just complete nonsense.

He puts his phone away and ventures into the kitchen to forage for anything edible for breakfast. He remembers having had another of his recurring dreams. In this one, he's a kid again and is exploring the miles of woods behind his parents' house. He's looking for Billy, who has wandered off, as usual, and calling his brother's name. John carries a black plastic bucket with a black handle, and, as he walks, he continues to find red Lego bricks on the ground and put them into his bucket. By the time he emerges from the woods into his parents' backyard, the bucket is full of red Legos. He dumps it on the lawn and crouches down over the pile and then begins to assemble a human figure from the bricks while continuing to call for his brother. He awakens just as he is affixing the legs to the torso.

***

Later in the afternoon, after he has showered and resurrected, he picks up his phone again and sees a private message from Janet. She writes, "Hey. I didn't want to post this publicly, but I thought you should know that Will was in the bathroom this morning with the kid who shot himself. I haven't told Mom yet, for obvious reasons. Will walked in just as the kid was pulling the gun out of his bag. He even said, what are you going to do or something like that, but the kid just walked past him like he didn't hear him. When Will left to go find a teacher, he heard the gunshot. It's just so terrible. All I can think about is us when we were kids, about you and Billy, and I can't stop crying. I'm sorry. I love you."

That night, he and Ning stay in, and John passes out drunk on the sofa around 11:00 as Ning streams a full season of some TV series about stone-faced fashion models in Singapore. Ning knows about John's nephew's connection to the shooting but not the full extent of what's bothering John. As John snores with his face pressed against the sofa arm, Ning turns up of the volume on the TV to drown him out.

That night, he dreams he's at a massive outdoor carnival with his whole family. It's another common one from his oneiric repertoire. His mom and dad walk ahead pushing Janet in her stroller. He and Billy have stopped to play a game in which you shoot bottles with a rifle to win stuffed animals and are now running to catch up with their parents. John looks down and notices he's still carrying the black rifle, which he must have inadvertently taken with him. He then notices that Billy is no longer running beside him. He stops and looks around, calling Billy's name. His parents are now so far ahead that they're out of sight, and he knows he'll be in trouble if they discover he's lost his little brother. He stops and scans the vicinity for any sight of Billy. Then John spots his brother off in the distance smiling and waving while holding a string tied to at least thirty red helium balloons. John laughs and runs towards Billy, still clutching the rifle. Suddenly, Billy lifts off the ground from the upward pull of so many balloons and begins to rise toward the sky. John reaches to grab Billy's feet but narrowly misses them as Billy floats higher and higher. John then lifts the rifle and aims at the balloons to pop them, but by the time he has adopted a proper stance and taken aim, Billy has drifted too far aloft. Before John awakens, he sees the receding image of red balloons in the sky shepherding his brother somewhere far away.

***

On Sunday morning, John reenlists in the ongoing online skirmish over guns and gets into a few heated discussions with friends and acquaintances. Ning has gone with friends to a free-flow champagne hotel brunch, but John begged out, claiming he was going to chat with his sister or maybe call his parents.

To one friend, John writes, "I know there are many rational gun owners, and I'm sure you're one of them. Many of my friends and family members are. You're not out there yee-hawing and firing your stupid shoot-em-up toys all over social media, and, more important, you're not leaving dangerous weapons lying around everywhere for some moody, fucked-up little nobody kid to take to school and punish the world for failing to acknowledge that he's as exceptional as he's always believed he is."

To another he responds, "The status quo isn't working. It's time to try things, and if those things are new gun laws or metal detectors or goddamned Robocops menacing the school hallways, let's just stop talking in circles and do something already."

When someone suggests arming teachers to prevent future shootings, he offers, "Why stop there? I say you arm the TAs to get the drop on the teachers in case something goes wrong. Then, you covertly arm one or two of the kids as a last-ditch fail-safe. Not all of them, mind you; just a few, maybe from the gifted and talented register or any who seem unusually advanced."

He calls home that evening, which he can no longer avoid, and it's every bit as uncomfortable as he has expected it to be. It's mid-morning for his parents, and their A.M. concerns lie squarely with their traumatized grandson. So, they talk about Will and how he's holding up, and they're able to avoid the whole subtext no one wants to draw attention to.

That night, he stays mostly sober and, mercifully, is able to sleep without dreaming.

***

At work the next day, things are beginning to feel more normal for John. His colleagues seem more sympathetic than sanctimonious this week, and his first lesson goes really well. Ning sends him a few funny messages about bank gossip, and he uses his free block for lesson planning instead of social media polemics. He's become inured in these decades of dead kid ubiquity and better at not seeing himself as a victim. Or as a shooter.

At lunch, he decides to leave campus and walk up the street alone to a noodle shop. It's been a long winter, and it feels right to enjoy the warming weather on such a mild early-spring day.

Outside, he sees the students sitting at picnic tables and enjoying being outdoors. It's nice to catch young people acting so free and energetic. He's happy that violence is an abstraction for most of them, something only experienced in movies and TV shows as puerile entertainment. He knows there's virtually no chance of one of them pulling out a gun and slaughtering the others. No chance they'll have to hide terrified in a quiet, dark place to wait out the onslaught or have to call home and say a tearful maybe-goodbye to their parents. Or survive to become a tragic walking cause célèbre. He wonders if they realize how fortunate they are to grow up without this realm of possibility.

Feng wanders into his path and waves enthusiastically.

"Have a good lunch, Feng. Enjoy this weather and fresh air while you can. I think the AQI is going to climb tonight."

"Thanks. You too, Mr. McDonald."

As he walks away, John thinks back to his conversation with Feng the previous week. He feels confident he expressed the appropriate sentiments to the kid about guns and American gun culture, but he wonders if he should have been more honest about his own personal experiences. About his childhood. His father's hiding places. About guns. And, of course, about Billy.

The Plastic Age

by Douglas Alan Waltz

Georgie picked his way over the debris that littered the Southern California coastline. Ever since his twelfth birthday he had been one of many scavengers who came to pick over the bones of a large chunk of humanity that had been wiped clean by their own negligence.

Georgie had always been fascinated by the stories his grandmother told about the old days when Southern California was a densely populated area of the country.

That was until The Great Pacific Garbage Patch had made landfall in 2021.

The Great Pacific Garbage Patch had been discovered in 1997 by oceanographer Charles Moore. Believed to be primarily comprised of old fishing nets, it soon became apparent that plastic was clinging to the nets. Plastic discarded and sent out to sea. By 2011 the GPGP for short had become three times the surface mass of France.

People reacted like people always did; they did studies of the mess, analyzed the mess and had concerned citizens try to bring public awareness to the mess.

In 2019, a group of environmentalists were doing tests on the mass when something under the GPGP triggered a massive underwater explosion. Later it would be discovered that it had been a blue whale that had been infected with the radiation spillover from the Fukushima disaster in 2011. The bulk of the creature slowed the process of infection, but when the whale was migrating it became entangled in the GPGP and died of suffocation.

The explosion of the whale caused a temporary shift in the movement of the ocean and sent the GPGP hurtling directly at Southern California. According to Georgie's grandma the authorities did what they always did; they acted important and sent out experts.

That was their first mistake. Between the incident with the whale and the collection of refuse that had been collecting itself for no one knew how long something in the material that made up the GPGP had undergone a drastic change.

One of the scientists attempting to get a sample had a greasy black smear run along the back of his hand. He wiped it off along with most of the flesh of his hand and was dead in two minutes.

He had rotted to the bone and then his skeletal structure had collapsed from whatever was in the GPGP.

That sent a wave of panic throughout the state. Not only was every beach for miles about to be buried underneath piles of discarded trash, it held a disease that was instantaneously fatal.

For the first time in the history of mankind the state of California ordered a complete evacuation.

The Center for Disease Control was called in. They lost ten researchers before they discovered what they were working with.

It was like nothing they had seen before. The only silver lining is that it was not capable of going airborne. The military thought they could destroy it, but that was quickly shot down as if even a drop survived it would destroy any life form it came into contact with. And, if something died of it any contact with the pile of goo that remained would be capable of destroying anything it touched. It destroyed any form of life; plant, mammal, it did not care.

Ironically, plastic could contain it so they proceeded with a huge clean up as millions of people headed east away from the threat as ordered by the military. Blockades were put in place and orders were given; if you tried to get into California, you would be shot on sight.

The United States was taking no chances.

Georgie loved hearing these stories from his Grandmother. He thought it was fascinating that if it weren't for the GPGP he would have probably been born and raised in California. Now, no one lived there. When they finally managed to clean up the mess with minimal loss of human life they decided on a drastic form of disposal.

They were going to shoot it into space and set it on course with the sun. They were going to use the sun as a huge incinerator. Georgie wished he could have seen the three rockets take off into the California night. It had been a massive undertaking and the scientists kept reassuring the bureaucrats that the heat of the sun would destroy it once and for all.

He absent mindedly kicked a small plastic bottle that he came across in the overgrown city of Los Angeles. A small, hard shelled bug scuttled away when its hiding place was removed. Georgie watched the bug with fascination. Its black shell was so shiny it looked like an oil spill with its rainbow of colors when the sun struck it.

A small noise to his left made him look and he saw another figure walking through the dense undergrowth.

Not too unusual. Scavengers had their own code; you didn't mess with anyone. Sure, if you saw a scavenger in trouble you might help them, but it wasn't something that was done often. On this trip, Georgie's grandmother had sent him in to look for medicine. She explained that the bottles were plastic and she wrote down a list of the names he needed to look for.

After the GPGP had reached landfall and caused the resulting mess every country had left the United States to fend for themselves. Eventually Alaska and Hawaii became individual, independent countries. With zero foreign assistance it didn't take long to cause the collapse of the infrastructure of the country. Even the neighboring countries of Canada and Mexico barred entry into their countries. Mexico even constructed an actual wall with armed guards.

The United States was on its own and try as the government might they did not last long against the scared and angry hordes of the American people.

All of this had happened before Georgie was born. His parents had died when a raiding party attempted to take over their community. The raiders had been stopped and put to death and their supplies taken, but Georgie's parents paid the ultimate price in the process.

Raised by his grandmother, Georgie learned about the way the country used to be. He had wished he could have seen it. He could have been just another normal teenager, but his slender, agile form did come in handy when it came to scavenging. The barrier was still up around California, but it hadn't been manned for a very long time. It was cracked and overgrown and just stood as a silent reminder of the repercussions of the actions of a negligent society.

Georgie had managed to locate the building grandmother had called a hospital with little effort. He took out his crank flashlight and powered it up with a few fast turns. The orange light glowed in the dark halls of the deserted building. There were various, small noises that Georgie figured were rats. Rats loved California, but they still feared people. Georgie knew that was silly because the rat population outnumbered the people by such a large number that if they ever got it into their tiny brains to attack then the population of The United States would be gone. Just like that.

The hospital was fascinating to Georgie. In the six years of his scavenging he hadn't stepped foot in the giant building. Georgie preferred small places to do his scavenging. The bigger places were structurally sound, but the overgrowth was starting to eat away at the manmade materials. A building that size could crush him in an instant if it decided to come down.

Plus there was always the legend of the Californians.

Grandmother told him that some people were stubborn. The evacuation order was ignored and they decided to make the abandoned state a place of their own. Some people believed that their time in isolation had driven them mad and they had taken to the underground in the labyrinth tunnels of the subway to hide from the world above.

Georgie was pretty sure that the Californians were a myth. In his six years of scavenging he had met other scavengers, but never a race of underground dwellers. He didn't want to hurt his grandmother's feelings so he never mentioned it to her. She was an intelligent woman who had lived before the GPGP destroyed the country.

She had explained that she worked for a place called NASA. Georgie thought that travel to space sounded awesome and told her so when she described how she helped send people to outer space. As she got older she became obsessed with the three rockets that they had sent to the sun. Her biggest concern was that if the calculations weren't exactly right then the rockets could have looped around the sun and came right back to the Earth. She talked about it constantly, to the point that the other people in their village thought she was going mad.

Georgie had been a bright child and his grandmother made sure he knew how to read and write. He loved science and had an affinity for it. Soon, he was deep into his grandmother's books along with everything he could find about space in the small library that was part of their village. He understood what she was saying and it made perfect sense.

If any calculations were off then what she feared could eventually come to pass.

He managed to fill his backpack with thirty plastic bottles that had the words she had given him printed on the bottles. He could also see through one of the shattered windows of the hospital that night was falling so he called it a day.

He carefully made his way out of the hospital and went to the seashore. He loved to lay on the warm sand and look up at the stars on a clear night. He had been studying the stars and was picking out the Big Dipper when he heard noises coming from behind him. He carefully turned and saw a mass of figures slowly making their way to the beach.

Californians! Georgie thought to himself.

But, what could have brought them from their underground lair after so many years.

A whooshing noise made Georgie look to the sky and it showed him the answer.

Three large fireballs hurtling through the Earth's atmosphere towards the ocean.

Grandmother had been right all along.

Not So Tender

by Pete Chiarella

It was a really bad neighborhood: crack heads, junkies, hookers, homeboys, and Barrio Gangbangers. Not the place you would expect to see a blonde, very pregnant, young woman. But yet there she was, awkwardly walking by leering, drunken gang members, shouting propositions like you can't get knocked up twice. She was frightened, that was very clear. Julio was watching her pass by and was worried for her safety.

Julio was just a low level dealer. Not affiliated with any of the gangs, just selling bags of dope to stay solvent. When some of the jokers started getting grabby with her, he decided to intervene. Julio yelled at the bunch, telling them to back off.

"Is she yo baby mama?" one banger yelled.

"Just let her alone, ok?" Julio asked the guy, who made a big deal about rubbing his crotch, then walked away.

"If you need a place to crash for a bit, I live just around the corner," Julio told her.

"Why? So you can try your luck with me? I think not," she told him.

"Lady, you hang around here much longer, all you'll be is a story on the 6 o'clock News," Julio told her.

"Look, I mean you no harm," he continued "I just want to get you out of sight for a bit, you can book whenever you want."

She sized him up for a bit, and noted he was a good looking guy, no doubt.

"Okay," she gave in. "I'll hide out for a couple of hours."

He took her to his crib, a three room, rather neat apartment.

"You can crash a bit if you want," he told her. "I have some business to finish up, I'll be back later."

Julio went back to dealing. He was wondering if this chick was going to stay or just jet. He had nothing there worth stealing.

He kept his dope and his cash on him. Julio just figured he did his good deed for the year. \He came home fully expecting her to be gone. But she wasn't. And she wasn't pregnant anymore either. She gave him a smile. "Sorry," she said.

"Did you lose the baby?" Julio asked, concerned.

"There never was a baby," she said. "I just put some padding under my clothes. I thought that would keep the trash away from me, but I thought wrong."

"Well," said Julio "you're safe here. Are you hungry? I can run out and grab some food?'

"I am hungry," she said, "but not for food. How about I repay you for your kindness?"

She stood up and pulled her sweatshirt over her head. She wore no bra, her breasts were topped with strawberry colored nipples. She peeled off her jeans, and exposed a tight, athletic body. Julio quickly stripped, he was an impressive guy, lean with six pack abs. They kissed hungrily, tongues entwined, swapping spit. Julio sucked her nipples as she moaned and pushed his head down to her crotch.

"Lick me good," she ordered and Julio did as told. She moaned in orgasmic pleasure. She went to work on him with her mouth until he was rock hard, then guided him inside her. She felt like hot satin, she came a few times as he tried to hold back, but finally he was spent and collapsed on top of her.

"I hope you enjoyed that," she said to him. Julio smiled, exhausted. He went to pull out, but couldn't. Then he felt the pain, horrible pain that was pulling him tightly to her.

She looked up at him. "I didn't want it to be you. I was hoping one of the others would try me, but you did and that's sad for you because a girl has to eat. Julio looked into her eyes, eyes that changed from blue to yellow. He was being bent in half, he felt his flesh rip and his bones break. "You see," she growled "I'm a succubus, and I need to feed on the weaker of the species: the human male."

Julio's head was now touching his ankles, he was bent completely in half and was being drawn into her. "Goodbye, my sweet Julio - you sad fool." The last thing Julio saw was darkness as his head vanished inside her.

Twenty minutes later, a very pregnant girl was walking through the barrio.

That one Tuesday, when the beast came

By Mike Hammer

Gunner and Lincoln played their Kindles, they released beeps and tin can cries from a game where heroes destroy worlds. They sat side-by-side on the couch, playing the same game and watching each other. They both wore pajamas.

Harold Von Goldfish, their pet goldfish, sat on the shelf above the fireplace in the living room watching them, for seconds at a time.

Their dad, Rubix, walked in the front door, sweat dripping down his forehead, his red spandex suit clinging to his body. He held a briefcase. In the briefcase was a single apple for his lunch, the apple was rotten after having been in there, untouched, for five months or so. As he entered the living room he saw the boys and barked "Why aren't you boys in school?"

They answered in unison, without looking up from their Kindle screens or pausing their games, "It's Tuesday Dad. The Curse is on."

"Aaarrghhhh, I hate The Curse," bellowed their dad.

The boys were cursed to have terrible Tuesdays. Forever. They were 11 now and the curse showed no signs of slowing down. One Tuesday when they were babies they pooped so much it filled the kitchen. One Tuesday when they were in first grade their bicycles turned into spaghetti as they rode them down the street. One Tuesday in second grade they went to school and all the fire alarms went off, simultaneously, every time Gunner or Lincoln got close to them. Some small disaster like that happened every Tuesday.

The curse was Rubix's fault. He was engaged to Princess Catastrophe when they were teenagers. He was the top hero prospect in the country and she was the future queen, so their parents fixed it up early. Rubix met a girl during a hero mixer and fell in love, so he called off the engagement the Tuesday before the wedding. Catastrophe, who had some Witch blood in her, was none too pleased and put a curse on Rubix. It was only a minor Curse, a lifetime annoyance designed to punish him for breaking off the engagement so unceremoniously, but cursed his first born to have terrible Tuesdays.

As it turned out Rubix and the girl he met at the hero mixer – Ovo – did end up getting married and having kids, twin boys. Both boys ended up getting cursed. Ovo died when they were 5. She was crushed as her and Rubix battled a black bean monster. Rubix was left to be a single dad of young twin boys, he started drinking a bit, and moved him and the boys out to the edges of kingdoms, to less populated areas, where he could take less stressful hero jobs – draining lakes, rounding up alligators, stopping forest fires, stuff like that, and only fighting the occasional monster. The annoying Tuesday Curse posed less risk when Gunner and Lincoln weren't in populated areas. Plus, the morning commute wasn't very stressful. Rubix usually took Uber, already dressed in his Hero costume.

Today he had spent the morning running down some escaped pet squirrels and was sweaty and exhausted. He started drinking in the Uber ride home.

"Any Curse-related stuff so far today, boys," Rubix asked Gunner and Lincoln, as he came out of the shower, in a comfy pair of plaid shorts and his usual "I am the Hero, what I say goes" t-shirt.

"Yeah, we need new beds," sighed out Gunner.

"Well, new bed frames," said Lincoln. "The wooden frames of our beds disintegrated and turned to dust this morning, when we woke up."

"So, we will vacuum in your room later and go shopping for new frames this weekend, metal probably," said Rubix. "I'm going to take a nap before I make dinner."

Gunner and Lincoln continued to play their Kindles. A kangaroo kicked over cars on their screens. The cat, Dragon, sat next to them and meowed softly for food. The boys sat playing, mostly motionless, for the next two hours. They had huge smiles on their faces and chattered at each other in cryptic half words and unique lingo. Rubix tossed and turned as he napped, dreaming of battles he used to have. He woke up full of sweat, terrified of something he couldn't see in the dream, a big dark presence with a strange silhouette, like two animals mashed together. Rubix got out of bed to get a cold shower then made bowls of cereal for dinner.

***

Wednesday morning everyone had cereal for breakfast and the boys went to the bus stop to go to school as Rubix was driven to the office by his usual Uber driver.

The week was relatively quiet. Rubix took a few more difficult jobs and got a plaque for community service, the boys struggled with math classes. Wednesday night Lincoln invented a beast that haunted their bedroom - after seeing a raccoon outside some nights, and hearing it attacking the garbage can outside, below their widow, on the driveway of the house and seeing shadows of their cat Dragon some nights. A huge silhouette of Dragon would dance across the walls as Dragon passed in front of the eerie light shining in from the bathroom night light, and mashing together the shadow of Dragon with the sound of the raccoon Lincoln decided the most awesome pet ever would be a combination of a dragon and a raccoon, a drageroon.

Gunner was skeptical. He thought the pet might be too big, or fire-breathy, and what would it eat. The two boys spent the week drawing out the drageroon, starting a small unstructured, unfinished drageroon comic to figure out how exactly it would look. They planned it out as a raccoon-sized beast, with hair and wings, along with a snout that curves up a bit at the end. Thursday night they decided a drageroon breathes fire in small amounts. It had mostly orange fur, with some subtle yellow stripes along the sides of the body. The drageroon had four legs but walked mostly on its hind legs, however it did like to pounce on all four feet to break stuff. Saturday, Gunner and Lincoln sat across from each other at the kitchen table, a plastic bucket of crayons and markers between them as they sketched the drageroon feasting. A drageroon diet consisted strictly of blueberry frosted pop tarts and 300 gallons of milk a day, give or take a gallon, so it was definitely an intensive and impractical pet.

Sunday night the boys couldn't sleep because of crickets chirping furiously and they decided a drageroon sounded like a lawnmower when sleeping, so you had to keep it entertained 24 hours a day. However, if you had one, you could teach it to be quiet to be snuck into classrooms or small areas to attack when needed. Monday afternoon, when they finished their homework, they sat around the kitchen table, sketching side-by-side and found a drageroon face was kinda of like demonic baby, an ugly kid with fat cheeks and purple eyes, and sometimes it wore a soldier's helmet, but not all the time. Gunner and Lincoln could not decide on a real great method to regulate helmet wearing.

Tuesday morning they tried not to wake up. They wondered if they slept through the day would the Curse go away, or happen anyway, or move onto Wednesday. They hadn't really tried that before. But around noon they could no longer fake sleep and were bored. So they tentatively ventured outside. They got their bikes and were riding through the neighborhood when the ground started shaking. Gunner jumped off his bike. Lincoln turned back to watch him. Gunner landed fine, didn't break a leg or twist an ankle, but the sky above him became an orange fireball, and there was a hairball growl like a clap of thunder. Lincoln fell off his bike and landed next to a smashed dead bird on the road.

"Oh my God," yelled Gunner.

Lincoln sat up in the middle of the street and followed Gunner's eyes. The boys stared at a furry orange beast standing on hind legs that were as big as Redwood tree trunks. It had smaller front legs that were curled up at the chest and reminded them of a T-Rex. The beast blew fire up in the air then jumped, the boys screamed as the drageroon flew overtop them and landed, extending the front legs, on all fours, on top of their house. The drageroon flapped the little tiny wings on its back then hopped on another house and continued going west.

As the boys stood slackjawed staring at the beast hopping

away a police car pulled up beside them. The cop in the car rolled down the window to talk to them. They didn't move and kept their eyes locked on the drageroon.

"Shouldn't you boys be in school," the cop asked them.

"Our dad is Rubix," said Lincoln.

"Rubix the hero? His kids still have to go to school," the Cop said.

"Not on Tuesdays we don't, we are cursed," said Gunner.

500 feet in front of them the drageroon knocked over a water tower, both boys winced as they watched it fall.

"Don't you wanna call the hero council or something," Lincoln said to the cop.

The cop finally turned to see what they were looking at, the reason they never looked toward him or moved their eyes, and he saw some huge furry thing trying to fly, but just hopping and landing on buildings.

"What the hell is going on there? I guess I should call in some heroes," the cop said, and got back in his car to get on the radio.

Dispatch told him the hero council and most heroes were at a retreat on an island in the South Pacific Ocean. It was an unplugged retreat, so nobody had cell phones or computers or watched TV for three days. He asked for a helicopter to fly over the southwest part of the city to check for some damage. The reports came back that there was a five story tall half dragon half raccoon beast making its way west, southwest, and destroying stuff it landed on, or stumbled over carelessly, as it moved along. Emergency announcements were made to get people out of harm's way and kingdom security command guessed the beast was headed toward Princess Catastrophe's castle. Rubix was one of the few heroes still in the country, since he had children to take care of, and he was taken off his zoo repair job and sent to the castle.

"Well, I guess your dad won't be home for a while, you two head home, and stay out of trouble," the cop told Gunner and Lincoln, before he drove away.

The boys rode their bikes home and found their house

crushed. Most everything was destroyed by the giant footprint that came down through their roof.

"Great," Gunner said. "Dad is supposed to take care of us and they send him away."

"Let's knock on Mrs. Crabtree's door again, I guess," said Lincoln.

The boys dropped their bikes on top of the rubble that used to be their garage and walked across the street, looking solemn and hanging their heads.

Dressed in his red spandex, which hid the BBQ sauce he dropped down his chest, Rubix sat in the servant's kitchen at Catastrophe's castle feasting on BBQ ribs.

Catastrophe came into the room and fired a cold stare at Rubix. He licked his lips and stood up, knocking down his plate and cup.

"Princess. At your service Princess," he mumbled.

"They tell me some kind of beast is heading toward me and may attack the castle," she said.

"It may not, m'lady. It may just keep moving on. I am here to stop it if it does attack," Rubix said.

"Do you know what the beast is and how to overpower it?" Catastrophe asked.

"M'lady, I fear, from the reports, and since it is a Tuesday, and since I talked with my sons earlier, I fear that, maybe, it's possible that um…"

"Spit it out Rubix."

"I think it's a drageroon, a half dragon half raccoon that my sons made up and drew this week. They think it came out of their imagination and crushed our house and ... and ... it's all your fault, it's all cause it's a Tuesday and you put that Tuesday Curse on them and you're paying for it now. You reap what you sew Princess," said Rubix.

"How dare you. You stood me up, if you hadn't…….."

"You put a curse on innocent children, just 'cause you were unhappy. You didn't even love me. And now I think the curse is getting stronger if they can create beasts just thinking of them."

"Well I, um… that does happen with some curses, they do evolve over time, hmmm"

"Princess, please, if this beast travels here, and I kill it, and save your life and prevent damage to your million dollar castle, will you please end this curse and let my sons be normal," begged Rubix, dropping to his knees.

"Rubix, I can't…. You… Fine… if you slay this beast, even though you are just doing your duty, I will lift the curse on your sons."

The guards at the top of the tower radioed down to Rubix that the beast was in view. Rubix smiled at Catastrophe and went out to meet the beast. He didn't want to be too close to the castle in case the beast was breathing fire. He cleaned up and washed his dishes, put a six foot rib bone in his back pocket, put the leftovers in the fridge and was outside in front of the beast in three seconds. Rubix stood staring up at the drageroon in an empty field about 300 yards in front of the castle. The drageroon breathed softly, smoke coming from its nostrils. Its eyes flashed green and purple alternately.

Rubix ran at the drageroon's toe and stuck the rib bone thru its pinky toe to hold it in place. The drageroon bellowed, loud and unhappy, then jumped, ripping the bone out of the ground as it raised its foot, and tried to land on Rubix. Rubix darted to the side and the beast landed in a cloud of dust next to him. A moment later a stream of fire came out of that dust, toward Rubix. Rubix darted away again, only slightly singed. He pulled a tree out of the ground and went at the drageroon's foot again, This time the drageroon kicked him away, shuffled its feet trying to crush him and then breathed more fire at him. Rubix darted between the beasts legs and grabbed it fury tail. The beast wailed as Rubix grasped onto the tail, wiped some BBQ sauce from his outfit onto the drageroon's tail and bit the tail. There was a tree-shaking caterwauling from the beast and it reached back to hit Rubix, but couldn't reach. The drageroon swung its tail under its chin and breathed fire at Rubix, but Rubix darted away and the beast set its own tail on fire. As the beast floundered, Rubix poked it in the eye, he sat on the beast's foot and pulled the rib bone out of its pinky toe, then shoved it in the eye he had just poked. The drageroon was rolling around now to put out the fire on its fur. Rubix skitter-skattered, to avoid getting rolled on, darted to the side of the beast, tore another tree out of the ground and started beating the drageroon. But, soon the fire was out and the, now one-eyed, drageroon simply looked pissed, and Rubix was getting tired.

The beast and the hero stood facing each other. The drageroon flapped it tiny wings then leaped forward at Rubix, with all four feet kicking at Rubix. Rubis slipped to the side and the beast missed, falling onto its back, Rubix jumped on its stomach and the drageroon giggled. Rubix jumped again and the drageroon laughed more, then Rubix started to tickle the beast's stomach, which made the drageroon laugh furiously. As it laughed, the drageroon breathed a bit of fire with each giggle. Rubix then started to rub the half dragon half raccoon's stomach until the beast began to purr and eventually fell asleep.

After rubbing the drageroon's belly and making it purr and fall asleep, Rubix didn't want to kill it. He left the drageroon, quietly, and worked out a new deal with the Princess – she would still lift the curse, if he took the beast back with him to be a pet for Gunner and Lincoln. On the phone Gunner and Lincoln declared it an impossible pet, and said they kinda liked skipping school on Tuesdays, but they relented in the end and agreed to take the drageroon as a pet.

Rubix whispered sweet nothings to the drageroon, gained its confidence and coaxed it home. When he got home he found Gunner and Lincoln sitting in the rubble of the house, because they had annoyed Mrs. Crabtree so much that she kicked them out. Rubix saw the house was indeed unlivable and unfixable, so he and Gunner and Lincoln and the drageroon set out to find an island to live on - an island that had a good school systems, needed a hero for light duties and would have enough room for a friendly one-eyed, eye-patch wearing beast.

Passing

by David McCoy

pole vaulting
over

her home
Riga,
at
15 feet

slammed into

her

husband Rick

The Mayor

by Perry M. Phillips

I look for the hidden meaning in every sentence. A salary involves devotion and deadlines. Lately, I count replicas of the Mayor to fall asleep, obsessed by dreams of mannequins driving bulldozers. Another pastime involves the construction of amortization tables of our city's geometric decline. Three short years ago, I reported my findings about the current social crisis to the Mayor's Office but have yet to receive a cogent reply, only a brush off, knock-off, off-putting excuse for thoughtful consideration. I always follow cold leads. Hence, my discovery that the mayor's true concerns are not of the people has led me to further actions. I sent the city council and the mayor's legal team a 50-page report detailing his misdeeds, chronicling his history of drug and alcohol abuse, and exposing the shady financial power plays that so frequently go with executive turf. I received in return a 'notice of surveillance.' Proving in a court of law that the Mayor's behavior is not in the public interest is more difficult: Unmitigated, unlimited litigation. Additionally, I sent a copy of my report to the Pocket Press. I also included in the package a special video documenting the Mayor's encounters in the prostitute zone. Not even the city council foresaw that liberalizing "sexual favor" laws would merely grant the Mayor new legitimacy.

Two of my colleagues have agreed to pursue the legal groundwork for impeachment. Word of their work leaked; death threats followed. They have taken refuge, mistakenly I believe, in the tax assessor's office. Their thinking, if I can cut it to one sentence, is that they cannot be seen where they are not understood. This is not true for theorems, but perhaps people are different. In any case, it appears my colleagues were overwhelmed by abstract notions and failed to consider the Mayor's omniscience. We all make mistakes, are taken down more frequently than not. I, myself, read between the letters. I also know about false reports of avarice that the Mayor wore on his lapel. The Pocket Press is under his left thumbnail. Never do those papier-mâché wordsmiths say anything that would hurt the Mayor's feelings. Meanwhile, the Mayor has speed bumps on his face and bristles with vengeance. I continue to sleep in short, fitful segments, imagining my capture, capitulation, and decapitation. My abundant legal documents concerning the Mayor made a nomadic lifestyle impossible, and I am now in a secret location preparing what may be the only serious legal case challenging the Mayor's authorization of his vast repertoire of vices. Any groundwork for impeachment must be engineered carefully. The Mayor has a clever legal team. "Has the Mayor," they will ask the chief of police, "done anything illegal?" I have the task of showing the treachery in which the pampered city council changed the laws concerning the modification of city ordinances long after liberalizing penalties for capital offenses. In the interests of justice, I have randomly installed hidden cameras in city hall bathroom stalls. Video production on drug and sexual practices of city council members is under way. Briefs on city councilors are being assembled, letter-by-letter, and page-by-page; biopics are in post-production. This, at least, is a beginning. I have taken steps to light the way for those attorneys who follow should my location be discovered.

That the Mayor fall and fall hard is not what the people want. No one is spiteful about his transgressions. We all respect the Mayor for who he is, not what he does. His choices are ones we might make if, in his position, we had the audacity and immaturity. I say immaturity because the Mayor's crimes often involve prank and a gratuitous flaunting disregard for the very laws he proclaims to uphold. His recklessness causes our social fiber to unravel into a chaos that, in turn, may trump our orders. Never once have I claimed moral superiority to the Mayor. I merely ask the question, "Has the Mayor had his turn?" In a legal sense, I am preparing his resting place, and it is not for money that I do this. I realize that I am, in a sense, the Mayor's lint, clinging to his steel-toe slippers. However, I am also the future spark in the Mayor's hollow, mechanical heart where his vapors of nitroglycerin accumulate.

Never do I let him forget me. I send him notes daily. In this way, I act as his best adviser. No doubt, he finds our relationship a badgering annoyance. Further, I am all too aware that the Mayor has offered a reward for my head, just as his ruling predecessors might have done in earlier historical periods, issuing an edict or a 'wanted' poster for an enemy of the state. How can I feign surprise? However, first, I must be found. I have become adept at changing my identity even though I must maintain a close proximity to my voluminous files. Perhaps it is too easy to laugh myself asleep imagining the Mayor's crazy threats carried out upon my mortal body. He has publicly declared his intention to see my corpse become the feeding trough for a thousand red, white, and blue pigeons. I saw his steel-blue face on a 100-foot monitor in our town square, beaming with glee as he described how my body would lie cold and motionless, drained of blood, staring face up with my dead eyes open while his pigeons feast on imported bird seed tossed upon my cadaver by blonde Webelos.

The Mayor is a sick man, yes, but he has doctors. He is thereby assured that someone cares. Additionally, a man in control needs drugs to function properly. No one wants the Mayor to be unhappy while exercising his omnipotence. Further, we all worry how much worse things might become if the Mayor suddenly falls ill, creating a power vacuum. No one wants to see roaming gangs, now gainfully employed by the Mayor, gnawing on the bones of some tourist caught wandering unaware of our city's plight.

It is true that the Mayor has made public transportation safer and has succeeded in chemically removing old chewing gum from our sidewalks. Every citizen feels pride at these accomplishments, victories that can never be taken from us. We forgive the Mayor for his peccadilloes because he represents our ideals, fallen as they are, and ultimately, he is merely a reflection of our own weaknesses. As a city practicing democracy, we continue to actively vote and re-elect the Mayor term after term. Not only does it bring out his bashful side, but he is sometimes inclined to give out free prizes to lucky winners. He is very popular except for a few smoldering barrels who missed their shots and are now dead. Even when asked in our frequently recurring polls if the Mayor is Excellent, Above Average, Average, Below Average, or Poor, my answer is always Excellent. I really mean it.

This is why, in my legal efforts, I merely refer to 'the Mayor.' It is not the *man* who I am attacking, but the *position*, not even the position so much as the essence of the historical moment that has produced our crisis. The nature of the crisis is apparent to almost no one. Problems, we have learned, can be ignored more than one lifetime.

"Good Mayor," is a greeting frequently heard in trendy cafés. It is just the same as saying, "Yo," or "Sup?" Our language is changing to suit the times. This is nothing strange or horrible; language is a versatile tool of communication. All this is a major tenet of my case that the Mayor's popularity is in one-to-one correlation with the severity of the crisis. Indeed, the depth of the problem is now morphing the vernacular to adapt to bizarre circumstances. For example, the Mayor's title is often inserted into a sentence to normalize it, make it official: "If you're going shopping, get me some cigarettes, the Mayor is impartial," which is to say, the brand does not matter.

My case's psychological argument absolves the Mayor of all guilt because, in the end, he is an expression of our collective consciousness. This is why I want to see a pardon for the Mayor; he is merely role-playing to amuse us. It is true that some statistically insignificant number of people have died trying to assassinate the Mayor: all for show. Personally, I am not vindictive about anything the Mayor has done. Not even that escapade with the bulldozer and the nursery school. I would just like to see someone else get a turn. Of course, even my prodigious legal efforts will be nothing more than an invitation for the Mayor to voluntarily step aside. He might do this merely to escape the responsibility of omnipotence. I can imagine that day by putting my feet up on my desk and lighting a cigar... a cigar so sweet.

Good Neighbor Rich

by Dr. Rhonda Baughman

"You see it?" I whisper into my phone.

"I do," whispers Rich.

"You're a good neighbor, man."

"Quiet, now," he says. "Let's just watch a moment and see what they do. See if they make the first move." Good Neighbor Rich always knows what to do.

It's after midnight, Christmas Eve Eve. There's a light snowfall, a gentle dusting on the ground, and I'm surrounded by moving boxes. Boxes I'll be loading into a van in the morning before I begin the cross country drive to my new job in my new city – new frontiers all around. But my hometown knows it might not see me again for a bit and its reluctant to let me leave - hence this gigantic blue 4x4 idling in my driveway, interrupting the escape plan I've elaborately hatched. This monstrous machine is obviously some new obstacle, some fresh bullshit to keep me from getting a proper night's rest, which will make me tired and cranky in the morning from lack of sleep, and this will ruin my entire -

"Whatever you're brooding about, Randa – stop. The dome light's on," Rich says. "You have your piece?"

"I do," I say, not ecstatic to someone before leaving town for my new position which will, most likely, not involve shooting people but will entail disposing of them in other ways. So, if I have to clear out every motherfucker in the room, including my driveway, then so be it.

I can hear Good Neighbor Rich praying – my phone is alive with his voice in the valley of the shadow of death.

"And I will fear no evil for thou art with me," I finish with him, while clicking my Sig's safety to the 'off' position, grateful it's with me, too, along with the phone presence of Good

Neighbor Rich. He may be the pastor for a small Baptist church on the south side of town but right now he's also my wingman and partner pre-crime.

"Are you still watching?" I ask Rich.

"I'm still here. I won't leave you. Let's just wait a little longer, see if anyone steps from the vehicle. Scan for weapons. If you see none, try to establish contact. Don't just open fire. This is one of God's creatures, Randa. Also he's not in your house. Stay alert. He might not mean you harm. But if he does, don't hesitate to shoot for center mass.

"I know, I know," I whisper, grateful but barely recognizing my own rasp. Good Neighbor Rich educated me, quite well, on matters of faith, of destiny, of true aim. I would not do him the disservice of forgetting everything he taught me.

"Can you see anything?" he asks.

"Negative," I respond just as the door to the driver side begins to open. "Wait! Someone's getting out."

"Standing by," Good Neighbor Rich says.

And someone does exit the vehicle. The someone is a damn large black man. Seriously. He's huge. All round and blue puffy coat. I grip the phone tighter and squint through my blinds. The man appears to be looking at something in the vehicle, perhaps on the driver's seat. I relay this information to Good Neighbor Rich.

"Do you see a weapon?"

"No, sir."

"Do you know this man?"

"No, sir," I say.

The car is still idling. The man is in no hurry. If I had just gone to bed at a reasonable hour, I would have missed all this – and the man would have finished his business, stolen my car, perhaps broken in and slit my throat and I wouldn't have to be -

"Randa. Control your breathing. I can hear you. Take a slower breath," Rich says.

I know he's repeating my name to calm me. I do as he suggests and it works. Meanwhile, the man has finished on the driver side and moves toward the house. The motion light kicks on. The man blinks in the harsh spotlight, but does not run. And he seems to be whistling. Damn, I hate whistlers. This guy must be dangerous to be so calm, so smooth.

"He's moving toward the front door," I say.

"Be ready," Good Neighbor Rich says.

The man is almost to the screen porch door. I can't stand it any longer. I open the front inside door and speak in a voice not my own.

"What do you want?" I say and make sure he can see my weapon pointed directly at him.

"Woah, hello. You startled me," he says and he slips in the snow. "Hi, Ma'am. Uh, please don't shoot. I have -"

I cut him off. "Keep your hands where I can see them. I'll fucking shoot, I swear to God."

"There's no need, Ma'am," the man says and regains his balance. And he smiles, big and wide and deadly and I'm shaking and sweating and I don't want to shoot but I will. And I'll have to call the police and file a report and get a lawyer and stay for my trial and I will never get to my new job and flakes fall above us, around us, as if we're in our own snow globe, an inexplicable scene - no Wise Men here, but a biblical scene nonetheless.

The man's hands are in the air. "In my pocket, Ma'am – are the stickers. I wanted to place a red sticker on the mailbox. You're Sunday only now, right?" The man says and I have no idea what he's saying. There are words but I can't discern their meaning.

"It's Tuesday," I say and raise my weapon a little higher.

"You have a good night, Ma'am," the man says and walks backward to his truck, still smiling.

Good Neighbor Rich is speaking but I can't understand him very well either.

"... sticker! Red is Sunday only. Randa – be calm. Can you hear me? Don't shoot - He's a weekend paper delivery driver," Rich says as I watch the man drive away, erratically, knocking over my trashcan and hitting a patch of my lawn. Almost as if he was scared. Well, good, right? Tiny white woman with weapon scared large black man with the big ole' truck.

There's a weird headline.

"Randa! Can you hear me? Do you need me to come over?" Good Neighbor Rich asks. He's a great neighbor that way.

"No, he's gone. I think I scared him away," I say.

"I should say so. Are you listening now? I think he was the delivering the Sunday paper."

"What do you mean?" I ask, my voice shrill and painful to my own ears.

"I heard him say 'red stickers, Sunday only'. That's one of the stickers that o on the paper box outside your house. Blue is daily, green is Saturday, red is Sunday." Rich says.

"What?" I ask, still full of adrenaline and terror.

"My son. He delivers newspapers. I sometimes help. The stickers are for the local paper," Good Neighbor Rich says.

I pause. I laugh. And then I begin to cry.

"You mean, I almost shot a paperboy?" I ask.

"It's all right, Randa. Most people are asleep by now. He probably had no idea you were awake and no idea he startled you."

"Oh, Jesus Christ. I almost shot the paperboy."

"Language, Randa. Thou shalt not take the Lord's name in vain. And to be fair, that was no boy. That was a very large man," Good Neighbor Rich says.

"And black," I say. "So, I'm a racist, too. A racist who almost shot the paperman." My adrenaline is wearing off and I can feel the headache coming in at my temples.

"You didn't shoot anyone, Randa. That's the point. A strange man, intimidating in size, was in your driveway at midnight. Give yourself a break. You're allowed to be rattled. But you still did great, I think."

Good Neighbor Rich is too kind. I now feel like a racist asshole who almost shot a man for trying to put a sticker on my paper box to make the route easier for a driver. I now see his midnight visit as someone cursed with working long, horrible hours.

"There are no bad guys here," Good Neighbor Rich says.

"Surely goodness and mercy shall follow me all the days

of my life," I whisper into the phone, clicking the gun's safety to the on position, resting it atop a moving box. I sit on the floor, my head on one knee.

"And we will dwell in the house of the Lord forever," Good Neighbor Rich says.

I hang up before either of us can say "Amen."

A Lack of Structure

by Clifton Boggs

I.

The closest thing to enjoy is the ramblings from a wise old waterfall. Chasing after itself time and time again. Slapping against the precious gemstones, beneath the water's fragile surface. Creating generations with riches to share or explore. Tucked, oh so perfectly into this dark, quiet cavern. Where history has danced all over these walls for centuries. Every movement it undertakes breeding new life. Yet, it seems like yesterday. Humanity placed it so perfectly with its own bare hands. Smoke fills the tight, small area. Lights reflect off the walls. As the shadows march calmly toward the opening. What we lose in the fire - we will gather from the ashes.

II.

Living on the third floor of this amazing structured building. Looking out into the abyss of farmland and cobblestone architecture. In the distance the canal murmurs softly on its way to the Black Sea. Encased with culture and shrewdness. Two partners set off for their journey of a lifetime. Some may say pure adventure. The trees gently blew in the wind. Blades of grass whisper against the private entrance. Tucked away on top of the world. A little piece of paradise. Which seems to remind the brain of comfort, of possibilities. Shuffling to make a quick getaway. Pouring in like the sand of an hour glass. We devour the cold, leather seats and crowd into the steel steed to disappear. Time lurks behind every foot step. Slowly reaching the dark tunnel - what could sit beyond fixation, at the other end, besieged by darkness.

Waking up, two silhouettes hovering over the foot of the bed. Masterminding the fate of my virtual surroundings.

Intentions to dash out the nearest open window. Escaping the stronghold which might fall upon extreme circumstance. Calmly settled by a confident gaze and affectionate touch to the lips. The point of contact rustles through the consciousness and straight down to the toes. Rocking the body like a thousand horses racing to the finish line. One of the shadows dissipates from the scene, coordinates everything from the expert's mouth. Still staring into the smirk with the vicious plan of attack. Baffled by the outcome.

Suspended from rooftops are handmade blankets. Against the barrio walls, woven baskets line the street. Miniature paper maché cutouts ride string waves from lamp post to light pole. Visually the colorful festivities are a personal Eden for guidance. Quickly, running into the vast crowds of informal folks. Each handing off a burlap sack insisting it's for the living. Cherish those close to your heart. Within seconds, running into a mob of familiar eight wheels archaic wenches. The adrenaline flows through my air like a raging bull. Parading the moment on the pages. Follow me. Hurdling through air while it gently molds our human imprint. The cantina reeks of vodka and the slight pungent stench of cannabis. Immediately losing yourself into someone else's soul - could be the only way to finish and start from the beginning.

Later

by Tom Meadowick

So this was it, eh? I must say I wasn't much impressed. I would have expected more, but it was actually pretty plain. Don't get me wrong, it was nice, tidy and big, very big; it's just, I was expecting something more. There were lots of people. In fact everyone was here. Well, nearly everyone. But it wasn't crowded and everyone was relatively happy.

Oh, sorry. I guess you're wondering what I'm going on about; "The afterlife"- of course. You know; heaven, paradise, the final reward, whatever euphemism you prefer. Did I forget to mention I'm dead? No big deal actually. I led a pretty good life and then one day I'm driving down the road, on a beautiful winter afternoon and a semi hit a patch of ice. Let me tell you, when a Ford Tempo and a Peterbilt go head to head put your money on the rig every time. So, the next thing I know I'm hovering above the scene thinking *Hey, how did I get up here?* It took a few minutes to figure it out and once it sunk in I felt kind of bad. Not for myself but for everyone else. They gave me a real good send off. There were flowers and friends at the calling hours. There were people I hadn't seen in years. What a shame that they didn't come visit while I was alive; still it was nice of them to show up at all. I guess you never know how popular you are until you're dead. All this time I had been accompanied by Fred, you know, to kind of show me the ropes. Fred was like my guardian angel, in fact I think during my life that's exactly what he was but he doesn't like to discuss it. Anyhow Fred was there right from the start showing me the dos and do nots of the afterlife. So when my body was finally laid to rest Fred escorted me here. I could have come immediately but I wanted to hang around a bit and Fred said that it was acceptable.

Like I said before, I wasn't that impressed. My first thoughts were mostly disappointment. No "Pearly Gates", no robes and beards, no harps and wings, no fluffy clouds. It was really not much different than earthly life, except for … well, the happiness level. Everyone was given one. You see there really was no heaven and hell, per se; there was only your happiness level. The better the person, the higher the happiness level. I guess this is going to be a hard concept to present because happiness is just so hard to define. When a person has a low happiness level it doesn't mean that they go around crying all day, or that they physically suffer in any manner, it just means that their capacity for happiness can never be filled. They can still laugh at jokes (yes, we still tell them … Two seraphim and a cherub go walking into a bar… never mind, you probably already heard it! Or will eventually ...) and feel good, they just can't be as happy as some with higher levels.

I guess the best analogy is comparing it to going to school. A child in the first grade, even a very bright child, cannot begin to understand third or fourth grade level education let alone college. They don't feel awful for it - as they are doing what they can at their grade and thus fulfilled: they just don't understand. So it is for those with a low happiness level, they will never understand and enjoy full happiness. The difference is that here you are aware of your level and what you are missing. So if there is a "hell" as such, it is knowing that you will not be able to attain a higher level of happiness than your current level. For some people it isn't that big a deal as even a level one is fairly happy. In fact during your average day most people linger somewhere around level three. It is only at certain events or special moments that the happiness potential rises. About the highest level I've come in contact with is a nineteen but I'm told it can go higher. I don't know why it would have a need. No one else knows what your level is although even I can pick out the level ones and level twos but anything above a three and I don't have a clue. Fred says he can recognize up to about a level six but after that even he can't tell. Not that it matters to anyone except the individual who has the level.

Let me also mention that your level of happiness in life is in no way connected with the level you get assigned here. A life of unhappiness doesn't automatically get a reward here nor does a life of happiness get a punishment. It is what you did with your life that gets you your level. I won't go into what level I am, suffice to say I feel it is more than adequate for my needs and that I must have led a better life then I'd imagined. We have no other real differences. Anyone can go anywhere and do anything they'd like with no restrictions. Again some enjoy things more than others as your happiness usually dictates how much you enjoy something but your happiness level does not restrict you in any other way.

One of the best things is everyone you meet, because everyone who has ever lived is here. My first few days were taken up with seeing relatives and friends who got here before me and catching up on things although they were aware of what has transpired on earth since their passing. When I say we can go anywhere it does include back to earth. We just can't interact with those who haven't passed to this side. We also get regular updates through a sort of news service. It covers everything from universal down to personal family updates. Even though my passing was rather unexpected, the relatives put together a fairly lavish welcoming party. Relatives I never even knew I had were there to welcome me and introduce themselves. It was very nice.

Getting around up here is great - all you have to do is think of something or someplace and you are there. If you want to go see someone you just think of him or her and you are there. Now I don't mean a passing thought - I mean you have to particularly think "I want to see ... whomever" or "I want to go … wherever" and you are suddenly with the individual or in desired location. Going someplace posed no problem right from the start, but going to see someone was a little intimidating because I feared just showing up in front of someone might be a little rude. Especially if the person was busy at that particular moment. But it turns out to never be a problem. Everyone is always happy to see everyone else even if they don't know you. And there is no such thing as a bad time as no one has to bathe, eat, sleep, or evacuate (look it up). We have all the time in the world so our time is not of so much a matter.

Something else I learned is that there is no such thing as "rude" here. I mean you can't be rude! Rude does not exist. In life I could be quite rude when I wanted but here I can't. I guess what I mean is I have not wanted to be and no one has been rude to me so I guess it doesn't exist. I've gotten to sit down and chat with some of the greatest people in history and they all treated me with courtesy and respect, even some of the ones that our history tells us were stinkers. By the way, Attilla The Hun's middle name wasn't really "The" but "Allan" - go figure. Anyway he was very cordial and quite happy to chat with me, which brings up another point: communication. Everyone speaks the same language, or at least understands each other. It is very pre-Tower of Babel here. I've met people from every part of the earth and had no trouble understanding them or making myself understood by them. I'm also a little unclear about personal perception but there seems to be some difference in it up here. It seems that we perceive and are perceived in different ways. What I mean is when I meet with someone I knew earth side I see them in the manner that I am most familiar with but that is not how others might perceive them. Example: my grandparents. I viewed them as I remembered them, a couple in their early 70s but I know for a fact that my uncle see them (his parents) as only in their 40s. Thus we perceive them as each of us remembers them. Now when you meet someone that you have no previous perceptions of I think you view them, as they perceive themselves. Even though I had seen many pictures of Leonardo Da Vinci I had no real, locked in, notion of how he looked and thus he looked considerably different than I might have thought. I can't help but wonder how I looked to him.

I guess you noticed that I haven't made any mention of the management of the place. By management I, of course, mean Supreme Being, and support staff. I guess that is because I was totally blown away by it. The Supreme Being is just that … Supreme! Just as you would imagine he is in total control and with the various "angels" they pretty much run things here. Since I was raised Catholic my conceptions are Holy Trinity and angels (Seraphim, Cherubim, etc.) but I believe that your spiritual background dictates the perception of these beings when you run into them. And that is another beautiful thing; you actually do just run into them sometimes. "GOD" isn't cloistered away meeting only with the high muckety mucks, he actually is out walking amongst the common folks talking, laughing, and completely at ease. It takes a little getting used to but after a while you are just as ease about it all as well.

Well, I guess that's about it. I've probably told you more than I should and let's face it, more than you want to believe, so I'm off to a party. One of my third cousin's will be arriving in about an hour and we gotta get the decorations up.

Don't worry – we'll get 'em up before his arrival. I was always good at hitting deadlines.

And wait 'til you see the party favors we have planned for you.

You're a Good Egg

by Panty Puzzle

Writer Biographies

Jason Simon is an international school teacher and short story writer originally from Canton, Ohio and currently based in Beijing, China, where he is the head of high school English at Western Academy of Beijing. He and his wife Jennifer have spent the past decade traveling and working outside the United States and have previously lived in Cairo, Egypt and Ho Chi Minh City, Vietnam. He writes primarily about the absurdities of American expatriate life and about looking back at one's own country from abroad. Some of his other stories can be found at https://medium.com/allpersonsfictitious.

Ilaria Easom is a British born, stubborn, fantasy-obsessed cancer survivor with a mind too big and racing too fast for their body. Currently a sophomore in Tucson High Magnet school in Arizona and the child of a British librarian, creative writing class is a firm favorite. Writing has become an addiction and a way of exploring ideas; just one world isn't enough to satisfy the runaway train of imagination contained in just under sixteen years of life.
https://www.youtube.com/channel/UCwdPQ43-yV6o937rqR-NF-Q

David B. McCoy is an educator in a township school near Massillon, Ohio. In 1990, he earned a graduate degree in Socialization and Personality Development from Kent State University. For 20 years, McCoy has run *Spare Change Press*, which in recent years has focused on publishing *Solo Flyer* and organizing poetry readings in the Canton-Massillon area. His most recent publications include *The Geometry of Blue, Prose and Selected Poems* (1995), and a chapbook entitled *Rice Fish* (1998).

Stew Miller has survived everything thrown his way – and soon, shall return the javelins.

Pete Chiarella is 42nd Pete – lovingly caring for his animal crew and masterminding mayhem wherever he goes.

Fred 588 lives and works and rules in the wilds of Arkansas.

Dr. Rhonda Baughman is a teacher who currently resides in Northeast Ohio.

Cliff Boggs is the proprietor of Eulogy Tattoo in Canton, Ohio

Perry Phillips has had previous stories published in two anthologies—*Good to Go: Short Stories West Coast Style*; and *Male Lust: Pleasure, Power, and Transformation*. Phillips was recently told by a physician that he has an "intermediate chance of death," to which he replied, "I don't know what you mean," a stock phrase he has drawn on heavily as an adjunct instructor—*always* with honesty.

Steven Santana knows Canton as well as the editor of this series. And Canton should thank them for staying.

Robert Beveridge: November 2018 marked Beveridge's thirtieth anniversary as a publishing poet. When not writing, he makes noise (xterminal.bandcamp.com) in Akron, OH. Recent/upcoming appearances in Pink Litter, Triadæ, and Welter, among others.

Douglas Waltz knows his squirrels, his movies, and his dead white dudes: A writer needs three things, experience, observation, and imagination, any two of which, at times any one of which, can supply the lack of the others." William Faulkner (1897-1962)

Tom Mohler is currently really into sharing the hard candy.

Tom Mattevi is the proprietor of Comics, Cards, and Collectibles in Canton, Ohio.

Tom Meadowick is the man who looks like Ryan Gosling in 'Drive' and sounds like Scott Lucas when he screams.

Constance Plumley represents the best of Akron, Ohio. Coffee and OCD are responsible for her many talents. Really.

Mike Hammer is the Prince of Northeast Ohio and we shall never forget it.

Artwork:
Panty Puzzle: interior eggs, front cover
Stew Miller: back cover fairy

34171502R00059

Made in the USA
Middletown, DE
24 January 2019